northwest edge

DEVIANT FICTIONS

edited by

LIDIA YUKNAVITCH
& L.N. PEARSON

two girls
PORTLAND/SAN DIEGO

two girls

www.cut-here.com

lilnub@aol.com

This book was made possible, in part, through the support of the Regional Arts & Culture Council.

NORTHWEST EDGE: DEVIANT FICTIONS / EDITED BY LIDIA YUKNAVITCH & L.N. PEARSON

PRODUCED AND PRINTED IN THE UNITED STATES OF AMERICA

2000

cover art/design: michael connors
book layout/design: l.n. pearson

FOR THE ONE,
THE ONLY, & THE MOST
WONDERFUL LOVER OF WORDS
IN SOUTHERN IDAHO
THE LOG CABIN

[illegible signature]
29 SEPT. 00

Paula Connor
on my birthday

Viva la
LOG CABIN!
— TREVOR —
9/29/2000

editors' note

Foreign Bodies

The routine is:

Tell the parents of the almost infinite adaptability of the infant gut.

The following are among the foreign objects which have been safely swallowed and ultimately reclaimed by natural means:

Open Safety Pin, Teddy Bear's Eye with 1-inch Wire Hook, Coins of All Denominations, Screws, Tacks, Hair Barrettes, Glass Fragments.

The teddy bear's eye was treated with the old-fashioned cotton-wool sandwich and arrived at its destination beautifully cocooned in that admirable protective.

Note:

Rectal foreign bodies: Almost invariably the input of sexual deviation. They need general anasthesia and an experienced rectal surgeon as some of them do inevitable damage as they make their invariably dramatic exit.

Vaginal foreign bodies: Commonly a forgotten tampon, but others are sometimes inserted by sexual deviants. Removal is simple.

Accidents & Emergencies: A Practical Handbook for Personal Use. Edited by R.H. Hardy. Oxford Medical Publications, 1985.

waiting	1	ALLISON OWENS
the viewing	4	DAVID PINSON
how and why I kaacked that guy from sugar ray	16	TREVOR DODGE
the freemans	21	STACEY LEVINE
almost plum	26	PAULA COOMER
reduction	38	VIRGINIA PATERSON
faust/faustus	41	LEON JOHNSON
the view: a diptych	54	DAVID SHIELDS
nocturnal	55	STEVEN SHAVIRO
strategies in the overexposure of a well-lit room	62	LANCE OLSEN
what it lacks	114	MEAGAN ATIYEH
seeking ursa minor	118	COLIN DICKEY
properties of language	132	DAVID SHIELDS
when good people do bad things	138	LA PUSH, WA EXPERIMENTAL WRITING & TYPING CLUB

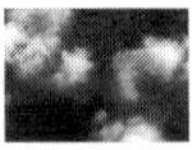

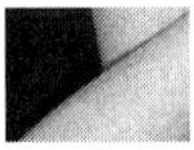

MICHAEL KROETCH 141 stopping time

BRIAN CHRISTOPHER 150 old school
151 the wait
152 evidence

ELIZABETH SHÉ 154 listening to mainie jellett

SHAMINA SENARATNE 158 crossing the marimba

DOUG NUFER 161 restraining order

BILLIE LIVINGSTON 170 I have this thing

JUDY MACINNES JR 172 another suitcase story

STEVEN SHAVIRO 184 abducted
186 blood

CHUCK PALAHNIUK 189 survivor

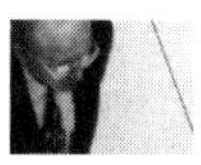

DAVID PINSON 202 seeping

BRIGID YUKMAN 204 child poems

DIANA ABU-JABER 211 the story of my mother's death: with a recitation by queen shaharazad

CAITLIN SULLIVAN 220 the egg

RICHARD KRAFT & L.N. PEARSON  –  little fires everywhere

waiting

ALLISON OWENS

Once there is a girl she goes to school she rides a yellow bus. She goes home. Everyday. She changes her grandmother's bedpan. Thursday her grandmother tells her she will pay her five dollars if she will shave Grandma's armpits with Dad's electric razor. The girl gets scared and calls Dad. Dad is Grandma's son. The girl lives with Mom and Dad and Grandma and Sister, in a house in a land far away from the village. Born in winter. What is the first thing the girl sees? Red rock. And something else, suspended.

On Sundays the girl rides in the car with Mom. They drive to the village and go to mass. Mass is in a church that is very old its walls are three feet thick its walls are mud. The girl picks a shape in the stained glass and stares at it. She looks at only one color and shape at a time, say lime green square. Then she moves her eyes to a new shape and color. When she is tired of this, the girl blurs her eyes and makes the colors bleed into one another. Lent is coming soon she thinks about Lent. On the last Friday of Lent, the girl and her sister must not speak from noon until three. Sit very still and look down deep into the carpet, imagine being inside it. Imagine spiders skittering under collar into ears, don't scratch it's not there . . . fingernails dirty again, little black crescents clean them it's Friday. The girl doesn't eat on that day. Only grown-ups fast. But the girl. The girl thinks about all this who eats and who doesn't who is forgotten. Remembered forgotten. Re-mem-ber. Three syllables accent over mem don't close the e's don't close the e's don't. Forty days and forty nights in the desert, tempted by a big black winged rodent. Satan was called Lucifer a long time ago. Lucifer is older than Jesus but at the same time is not. This puzzle makes the church spin while the girl sits very very still. When the girl is younger her favorite book has a picture of a girl on it holding a book, and on the girl's book is a picture of a girl holding a book, and on that girl's book is a girl holding a book and on that girl's book. . .

One morning the girl is eating something thick and grey. She chews it carefully, each bite. Her sister is quicker. Quick, can swallow without chewing. Sister gets to sleep later. The girl sits there by herself and listens to the radio, watches rabbits waking up in the hutch outside the window. A man's voice on the radio buzzes and at first she doesn't pay attention shivering warm at the back of her neck until she realizes he is talking to her so she slows down his words. Linda Lee Daniels.

Three weeks later two policemen will find her body under a bridge, and that is all they will find. The girl chews, contemplates, the rabbits in the cage scamper oh their water is frozen again, cold and dry. Mad rabbits bark and bite. Sister's dark curls cover the window she sits across from the girl and grumpily swallows two spoonfuls. Then they walk up the steep dirt slope, the same color as oatmeal chewed or left. The steep dirt slope is their driveway, it leads to the highway. The big yellow bus picks them up, they disappear in a cloud of exhaust and the neighbors' dogs chase the bus. The girl thinks about the highway follows it down past the school past the next town twisting through cholla snagged with transparent snakeskin, the watermelon colored rock, to the bridge where somebody took Linda Lee Daniels' body and left it. When people find her, her blood is solid her wounds like cafeteria Jell-O. Swollen and frozen but she did not die from the cold she did not die from the cold she did not die. The girl pries behind her eyes, finds rock frozen. And something else, suspended. Her fingers are black and brittle but deeper, hidden by layers of softest hair at the nape of her neck, the secret, waiting. The girl knows.

Back at the place where two highways cross, somebody had a choice. Two bridges equidistant, right or left. One choice leads here the other choice leads to the bridge a quarter of a mile past the girl's house.

In the afternoon, the same yellow bus creeps up the highway and lets the girl and her sister out where the highway turns to dirt. There are no more houses past this, just woods, so the bus turns around reluctant because it is empty because it has nowhere else to go. The girl and her sister walk down the hill in silence, go to the kitchen, eat cheese and crackers. Sister goes to Mom's room and turns on the television, lights up the walls the crucifix above the bed the puddles of change in the carpet. Strange music static humming, Grandma's noise leaks out from under her door and mixes with TV noise. The girl stops outside Grandma's door, listens, quietly sneaks down the hall. The girl puts her coat back on and goes outside. She walks over to the rabbit hutch which grunts and quakes, straw saturated with rabbit piss shakes loose from its wire floor. She tiptoes up and reaches in under the board on the roof her fingers barely touch bits of fur spin in her squinty eyes she pulls the bowl of ice out the rabbits lick feverishly at her fingers she is afraid they will bite jerks back and bowl slams against ground, hutch bangs shut rabbits seethe in snarling darkness. Bowl shaped ice lies at her feet. She leaves it there and walks up the driveway. She will go for a walk before it gets dark.

Past the curve where you could see through the poplar trees to the house, past Smokey the Bear blowing out a sputtering match that sputters forever even when it rains, past where the barbed wire fence runs into the ground. The girl thinks about colors as she sees them names them grey purple black green grey purple black green forest green no bottle green no mistle-toe green no she moves on the naming things rock pebble no dirt no particle no no no tree branch twig no stick no needle. She walks around the bend and there is the bridge. She hopes that the kidnappers are not waiting watching from behind . . . a tree no boulder no briar no *Smokey* no. Too many places to name now. She stands on the bridge toes chalked with dust sits on the low stone guard rail faces the road, looks everywhere but under. Quiet, only the wind funneling through the canyon walls above. The creek runs dry in winter. Just frozen rocks down there now. Just cold. Everyday she will make herself go up there and look, just to be sure. It seems so inevitable, like she is only waiting. Not breathing head tingling, get up and go down there LOOK LOOK LOOK.

the viewing

DAVID PINSON

I give the girl a quarter for the face to see if the glass has cut her palm, and to help her out some, as much as I may, I suppose, because of course she can not see. She carries three pieces of glass in the cup of her hand. Joined, the shards compose a face, and the girl displays the face—often slicing her skin—by squeezing the pieces into place. She does this for a price on the street.

"See the face," she says, clenching the glass in a fist and holding the fist to her chest while standing on the sidewalk. Her words are whispered background noise, almost unheard. "See the face." Plain, simple, soft. "See the face." A prayer, a poem, a phrase floating free.

People often walk away from the girl, step around her or add some distance to avoid. She is blind, and does not know this.

"See the face," says the girl.

To those who stop, she says, "You must pay to see the face."

Her name is Julia, and this is what happens when I say, "I pay to see the face." I place the coin gently on the center of her empty, outstretched hand, which in a flash deposits the coin in a pocket of her smock and remains there. I've decided the coin-hand, which is the grubby color of old metal, is the clumsier hand, and so is kept hidden during the performance that follows. Money safe then, Julia reaches out her other hand, turns it palm up and unfolds her fingers to manipulate the three shards of glass into place. She whispers yet another prayer as she squeezes the glass together for the viewing. What she says is "The face of God," and this is when I study Julia's wide, opaque eyes. Each time Julia whispers and squeezes the glass pieces together her eyeballs roll, and I suspect she is searching some inner sky for an answer.

A blacker picture I do not see.

So I purchase the face to examine Julia's white, hazy eyes to unearth an answer all my own.

Julia has memorized the placement of the glass. Julia's fingers are so deft at clicking the glass pieces into position to form the face in her palm that it is nearly impossible to study her movements there. She becomes a magician wrinkling a fat, silver coin across his knuckles, but of course it is not exactly the same, as Julia neither smiles nor yanks hares from a hat. Julia's only magic is the face.

"No questions," she told me the first time.

"But how do you know it's the face of God?"

Julia closed her hand and held it above her head. "Next!" she said. "Who's next to see the face?"

"You're bleeding, you know," I said.

And it is this bleeding—the continual spotting of Julia's blood—that attracted my attention. The hand underneath the face, I will tell you, is a web of dark, dried blood spots and scabs in the lines of the palm and the fingers. When viewers pay to see the face, they also pay to see Julia's crusted hand. It is my wish to touch this rough hand to my cheek, to lick it clean and then to care for this dear sweet girl.

But Julia will have none of me.

"I wish to see the face," I say each day.

She cocks her head.

"I pay to see the face," I say, and I set the quarter in her coin-hand, which squirrels my money down and away.

Julia says, "The face of God."

I hear this second prayer when sleeping. Julia's voice echoes in me. "The face of God," she whispers, and I go weak. I could weep, and often do, even when dreaming.

Julia is no beauty. No. No. No great shakes, but she has those eyes the pallor of a light bulb, and I stand closer every day.

"No touching," she said this morning.

"I wish to see the face," I said, and I poked my index finger again into her palm.

Julia drew back and wiped her smock.

"You must pay to see the face," she said.

"How about a freebie?"

Julia held the fist with the face over her head. She made a fist of her coin-hand, too, and held it above her head as well. Her wrists crossed, and I wished right then for a long wire I could bind her wrists with so I could hold her, just cling to Julia.

"Go away," she said.

"I'm blind, too," I said.

Julia stepped down the sidewalk. "Go away," she said.

"Julia," I said, "I will pay to see the face. I must see the face. I must see the face today."

Though of course it was not the glassy face of Julia's god I wished to see, but Julia's face. Yes, let's not be silly about this, dear ones, we know all too well I desired the face with clouds where eyes should be.

"You're not either blind," Julia said.

"Not quite," I said.

A big silence then.

"Who are you?" Julia said.

Who am I?

One sad man.

Julia walks with her arms out into my room. I lead her to a chair. Her hair is brown or black, inconsequential. Her smock is green and stained. I provide coffee and sticks of sugary gum, and she drinks from my favorite plastic mug. She says the room smells of must and sea salt. I think of dirty sheets and untapped windows.

I sit beside her. "Where's the face?" I say.

"Here," she says, "in my hand. The face lives in my hand."

Of course it does.

Julia has purpled shins, poor socks and thin shoes. I see the face-hand between her legs, and decide her legs are the arms of a tall, strong man who works under automobiles for a small wage.

Her chest is another matter, nearly flat under the smock.

"Fresh coffee?" I say.

Julia shakes her head more than she should, and fine flakes of skin fall from her hair. Her eyes resemble low-fat milk, and I deepen my mission to own them.

"You cold?"

"Not really," she says.

"Afraid?"

Julia hunches her shoulders, and sips from my mug. The coin-hand in motion, she sets the mug on the table and then pats slowly around the table top until she reaches a gum-stick. Julia unwraps the stick, folds and pinches it and then places it on her tongue. She chews, and then she speaks.

"Are you watching me?"

"You know I am," I say.

"You must pay to see the face," Julia says, and she laughs, the first time I have heard her do so. It is sharp, nasty and a knife into my ribs. Julia rocks back and forth, chirping. The face-hand—a fist still—comes up and covers her chewing, laughing mouth where there are rows and rows of smoky teeth. There is no smile on Julia's lips. Only a crinkle.

I say, "I wish to see the face."

Julia says, "The face?"

"Yes, the face."

Julia sips again from the mug. "Later," she says. "This coffee tastes of toenails." And she combs the coin-hand through her hair. "So I guess you want to fuck me, too," she says.

I am watching her eyes. There are light-black rings where the irises should be. Granite is the stone I am thinking of when Julia says what she says.

"What do you mean?" I say.

Julia chews her gum all around her mouth cavity. She says, "Every boy I know wants to fuck me. They say, 'Let's fuck the skinny blind girl!' Is that what you want to do?"

I realize I am staring. I realize it doesn't matter.

"Why don't you wash your hands?" I say. "There in the sink. Go ahead. Take a bath if you want to."

Julia says, "Look at me."

I already am. I watch Julia's face, watch the coin-hand slip from her scalp, watch the coin-hand reach out to my face, feel the fingers against my chin and her palm cup my cheek. Her hand smells of a bad shade of brown. She drifts two fingers over my nose and eyelids, which I close. She taps on my forehead, and I open my lids and find myself reaching up and taking her wrist in my hand. I kiss the palm where I set my quarters. I run a finger up her arm and test the soft spot at her elbow. Her hand covers my mouth, and I feel as if masked.

Then Julia moves one of her fingers to my lips and slides it inside. I taste the finger. I rub my tongue on it as Julia skitters the finger across my teeth, clicking nail against enamel. I bring my hand back down Julia's arm, and I tug the finger from my mouth, and rest it wet on my cheek.

"Julia," I say.

"What do you want from me?"

I tell her I wish many things. I tell her to give me the other hand, to leave the glass pieces on the table, that I wish to clean her hands, to wash away the blood stains, scabs and grime, and to take care of her if she'll allow me to.

"Take care of me?"

I reach for the closed face-hand. I pull it toward me and place it next to the coin-hand, which moves to re-cup my cheek. My tongue licks the bottom of her fist, catching the tiny cuts there, the dried blood there, but still Julia does not open the face-hand closed around the glass. I kiss between each dirty knuckle.

I say, "Care of you."

"Why?"

I say, "Drop the face."

"Drop?" she says.

"On the table."

Julia pulls her hands slowly from my mouth and cheek. I see the face-hand is gripping the face harshly now. The skin between the knuckles is turning pale. "I won't let go of the face," she says, her hand above her head.

"It's only glass," I say.

"It's the face of God."

"No, it's not, Julia." I say. "It is my face."

Julia sucks air through closed teeth, moves her chest, fills her lungs. Her hands she wedges between her thighs and partially covers them with her clothing. I count the veins in Julia's arms. There are six or seven.

She says, "It is so God."

"No," I say. "It isn't."

Julia's cheeks are red, and I stand, carry the coffee pot to the sink, pour the cool coffee into the drain and listen to the gurgle. "You're right. It tasted awful," I say. Suddenly, I feel heavier, as though sand and dust has layered me, weighted me.

"Oh, Julia," I say, "I am not much of a man."

Julia adjusts her head to my location. Those eyes! I could swallow each one. I could do that, or hold them in the pouch of my mouth forever. I wonder at their temperature.

"Truth is," I say, "that I am not much of a man."

"How can you say such a thing?" Julia says. "How can you say that about the face? What do you know about the face?"

"Dear sweet Julia," I say, "I also am broken."

Julia stands, scraping back the chair, and says, "You're insane."

I say, "And you're blind."

After a moment, Julia returns to the chair. "I am not blind," she says. "I see everything."

"No problem then," I say. "What do you see now?"

"Open a window," she says. "I can't breathe."

I step to the window, pull the shade down an inch and then let it wind itself to the top of the ragged casing. I am glad Julia is unable to view my poverty. I unlatch the window and push it open. A sharp gust presses against my chest, and I step back into the room. Julia is up and moving, arms out, shuffling to the window. "Sit down," she says.

I find my chair, a chair not at all like one I'd buy, but one usually found in a furnished room on the top floor of a wooden boarding house. My chair is painted a thick yellow, and the seat portion is formed perfectly. I have two such chairs.

"I like my chairs, Julia," I say.

"What color are they?"

Julia stands at the window. The breeze is bluffing in, and Julia floats against it. Her eyes are closed and she smiles into the pushing air. If I did not know of her sightlessness I would think: My, what a pretty girl this is, leaning out a window with her chin up and her hands across her stomach, and the breeze playing tag and dodge with her hair and ears.

I close my eyes, too, and I attempt to feel Julia's power, the face in her hand, the eyes in her face and the wind at the window.

"What's it like?" I say. "Inside your head, I mean."

Julia hums for several seconds. "I can see you," she says.

"Really? What do I look like?"

"A boy," she says.

"What else?"

"Something difficult," she says, and I wait for her, feeling my heart beat twelve—no, thirteen times.

Julia says, "Pain."

"If I close my eyes, too," I say, "will I see it?"

"Oh, yes," she says, "close them now."

"What color is the color of pain?" I say.

"Colorless," she says. "Like everything else."

Julia breathes. If I could, and I may one day, I would place an ear right below Julia's collarbone to listen. I would hear Julia suck air in and out and the fluids flow inside her, and I would dream we were both perfect; me not so broken and Julia not so blind. Julia would lay beside me, her hands clean and empty. I would ask her not to move. I would ask her to remain as calm as possible, to give me time to sink her all in, to find my answer, to make sense of her. My magic would keep Julia with me. Yes, dear ones, Julia would be mine. Do you see?

I open my eyes, and Julia steps from the window, arms out. "I must leave," she says.

I move to the door. "No," I say. "You can't."

"Please help me outside," Julia says. "I must leave now."

"But you can't leave now," I say.

"But I must leave," she says.

"But I haven't seen the face," I say.

"No," she says, "you haven't, have you?"

"I must see the face."

"See the face," she says, and Julia's fist rises up to me. Blood is caked there, and her nails are an uneasy color of pink. The face-hand that I kissed and licked not minutes ago is before me and opening as Julia's fingers flick the glass shards into place.

For her, I whisper the second prayer, and Julia fully opens her palm like a flower unwinding. I look at her eyes that are now blue. Julia's eyes are a faint blue over white, and rolling. Julia is seeking the secret to the pain on her inner sky, I know, and I wish only to offer myself to her, to help her pay the price, and so I reach up my hands and press my fingertips against Julia's useless, blue-tone eyes.

They are soft, her eyes, and to the floor then the face of God falls away.

They often talked of when the fever came.

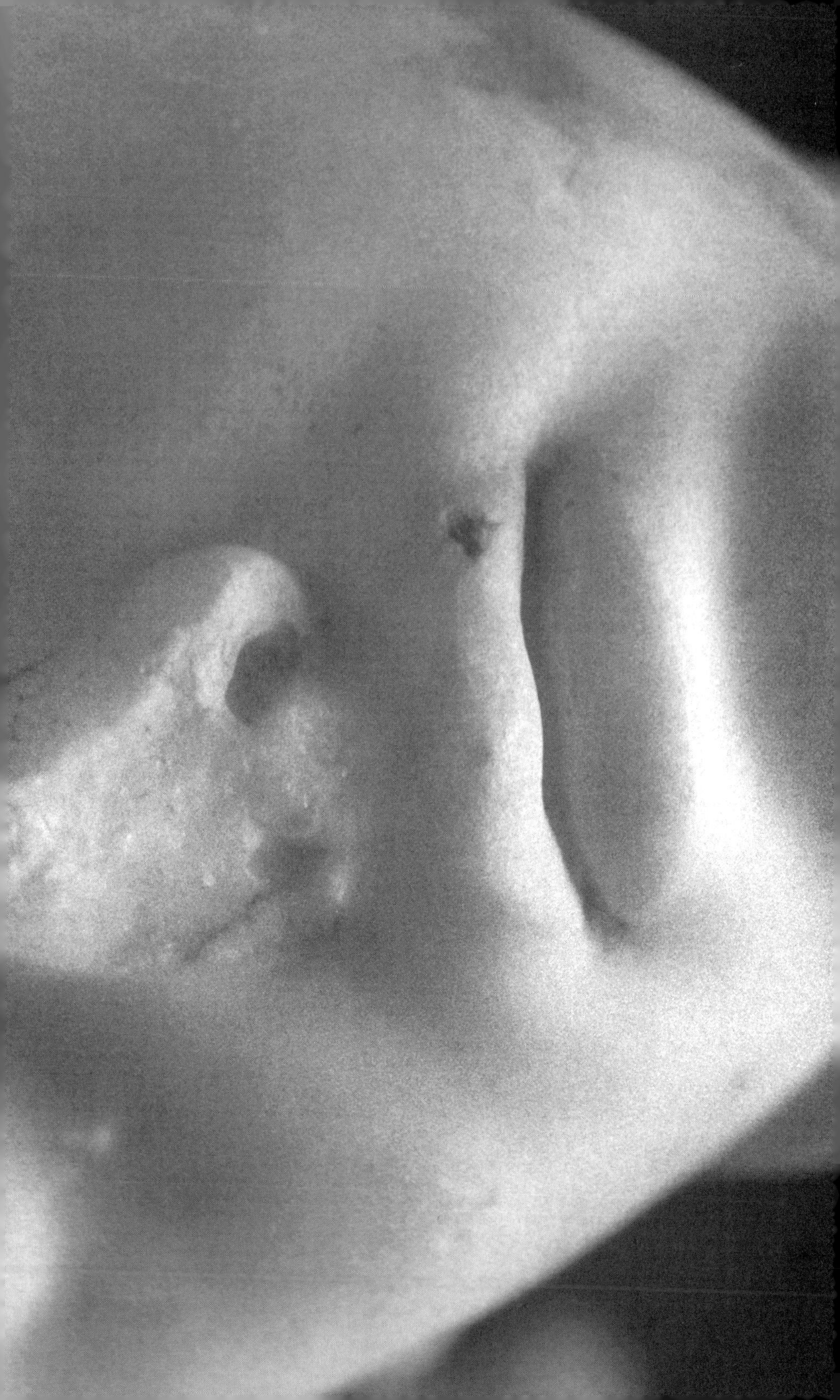

Everybody knew but no one dared to say.

Tomorrow she will say it was a mistake.

how and why I kaacked that guy from sugar ray

TREVOR DODGE

Oh yeah, I'd do it again. Over and over again. Just like this. You probably can't see that, that What I'm Doing (And Have Done), but I assure you it's really fucking gruesome. I have no problem Doing This, just like I had no problem Doing That to That Guy From Sugar Ray.

Sure. You say Why? You say What A Waste Of Two Lives, as if somehow my kaacking That Guy was, as you're implying, a completely selfless and cowardly act. I say this. You ever read Ayn Rand? Prima Movers? OBJECTIVISM/PO BOX 177/NYC NY 10157-0555, No Postage Necessary If Mailed In The United States?

Fuck yeah you have.

Officer Barbrady on *South Park*, Kellie Taylor on *Beverly Hills 90210*. You know you have. You've seen the $, the A, dreamt of Dominique Francon dressed up like the Invisible Girl, blue spandex, the works. Gregory Peck. Oh yeah. Filled your color-coded Zip® Disks with shots of Ayn working her post-Revolutionary body around Slavic cocks. The thick dark ones, worming their way into her Selfishness and spitting up on her stomach.

See, there was this kid in my eighth grade English class named Terrence McGrath. He did skateboard tricks off a Sherman tank in Harry Berry Park. Robb Roskopp, who is (or was) like the fucking king of rail grinds, flew in just to check this kid out. Yeah, Roskopp, the guy with the Bullseye Logo. So here's Roskopp standing right in front of the turret of this Sherman tank waiting for Terrence McGrath to do his ballyhooed Faceplant. Just waiting. Keeps waiting.

We're all like Just Waiting.

And finally Terrence McGrath shows up wearing these brand new Vision shorts with a big yellow dollar sign on the ass, yellow like a jar of Vaseline yellow, and he shouts, "Here's The Money!" and Roskopp has this scream wedged between his teeth because he can't believe he actually flew all the way to Twin Falls Fucking Idaho for this shit. This isn't omniscience. He actually says I Can't Believe I Actually Flew All The Way To Twin Falls Fucking Idaho For This Shit, parks a big lugey on the asphalt, and retreats to the Sno-Cone booth to use the phone. And there's Terrence McGrath with this cheshire grin on his face, not a thread of Roskopp on him, no Bullseye, not a single one of the four atomic orange wheels bolted to his board stamped with the initials RR. When the wood paneled station wagon marked up like a taxi lumbered off with Robb Roskopp in its backback seat, Terrence stretched his middle finger towards the sky and started walking home.

Let me ask you something. What did you do last night that made you famous? Did buying that 128 count box of Igloo Wafers at Costco make anyone take notice? Mopping up dog puke with a wad of paper towels? Pumping the car full of Premium Unleaded With 10% Ethanol For Cleaner Intakes? That's good for Everybody you think. Paying more for gas is good for the economy which is good for Everybody. Cleaner Intakes means cleaner air for Everybody. I'm bothering Nobody you think. And so you go back to Costco and there they are, Bothering Nobody Cargo Pants, and you buy them because buying them is good for the economy which is good for Everybody and you're still bothering Nobody. So you take your cargo pants home and throw them in the drawer with your Sickler chinos and Consumer Protection Ware slacks. And when you go to sleep at night you're wondering if there's nothing better than Costco because it's an Employee-Owned Store and how you vow to do all your shopping there because it helps knowing what you do helps Everybody and bothers Nobody.

Well it bothers me. It probably bothers Terrence McGrath too. To Hell With Terrence McGrath you're saying. Terrence McGrath

Painted A Dollar Sign On His Ass you're saying. And when I tell you that the last time I saw him that Terrence McGrath owned his own aquarium scrubbing business, you're going to tell me that Terrence McGrath Owning His Own Aquarium Scrubbing Business Is Just Deserves and you'll start humming a Gilbert and Sullivan tune as you drive away in your flashbulb white minivan. Because that bothers Nobody and you don't know Terrence McGrath and what Nobody knows won't hurt Them.

And To Hell With You Too you're saying. You Kaacked That Guy From Sugar Ray you're saying. And even though you've said it before you can't stop saying it because the way I disemboweled him with a curling iron hurt Everybody. Because the next time you're at Costco you find no fewer than 14 tribute albums dedicated to That Guy From Sugar Ray, Everybody from That Girl From No Doubt to That Guy From The Police lining up to recapitulate That Guy From Sugar Ray in digital clarity.

That's not my fault. Recapitulation aint my thing. See, recapitulation is this transitive action. That's not my fault either. I put little faith in things like the *Oxford English Dictionary*, collective projects trying to weed some semantic garden for Everybody. But they got this one right. Look it up. In 1768 H. Walpole writes in *Hist. Doubts,* "I will recapitulate the most material arguments that tend to disprove what has been asserted." If we're talking about Hist., let's fucking talk about Hist. already. Function of Hist. is to figure out how the present aligns with the past, to figure out how Terrence McGrath went from the Sherman tank to the fish tank, to figure out a confession can reify something like the gruesome, blistery death of That Guy From Sugar Ray. That's what *you* do. You're a fucking Hist.orian, right? Yeah see you didn't think so at first until I said it. That's the material argument, mofo. This aint a confession. Prophecy. Creation. Vision. I *see.* You *record.* And when you get done recording for the day (could you ever stop recording? of course not) you get in your fucking minivan, drive to McDonald's, and order your family their dinner in binary codes.

This is what I did today that made me famous. And you think I'm obsessed with being famous but I'm not. You think being famous is important to me, that being famous is Being Famous but it's not. It's just something I am. Something I can't help being. If you don't like it leave the fucking room already.

Alright.

The guy, That Guy From Sugar Ray, he's in My Chair today. Why I don't know. He's just in My Chair. Like he's slumming it I guess. I don't know. He's just in My Chair and I look at him in the mirror and he looks at me in the mirror and he keeps looking. In the mirror. Keeps looking. And I'm like spraying off the clippers with that disinfectant spray shit you know, waiting for him to answer me because I'd asked him already what he wanted. But he keeps looking. In the mirror. I'm like right in front of the fucker and he's bobbing back and forth trying to look at me in the mirror. I turn around to see what he's looking at and he's all Dude Stay Still and I'm going What Are You Looking At and he's still bobbing like a goddamn Weeble or something. So I say again What Are You Looking At and he goes Dude Stay The Fuck Still Already and when I turn around this time he grabs me at the shoulders and spins me back around and goes Dude I Said Stay The Fuck Still Already I'm Still Lookin and when I tell him to Let The Fuck Go he's still got his meathooks in my shoulders.

Then he just goes ahead and *says it.*

Hey Asshole Do You Know Who I Am?

You got pictures of the rest. I don't have to tell you.

No, I have no goddamn idea what That Guy was looking at in the mirror. And I don't care. Because I choose not to care. That was *his* business. And I had mine. It was a simple material exchange really, not something like a Pound Of Flesh or anything, but he offered it up just the same. Business. Beautiful. You ever hear anyone call business Beautiful? I assure you in its purest form, it is. No, you always hear people calling it Ruthless, Ambitious, Hostile. Never Beautiful. Not even Comely or Shapely for that matter, not to mention Homely, which is something you'd call the ugliest skag in your graduating class. Yet we rely on Business more steadfastly than our own fungus-infected feet. *That's* a crime. Not kaacking That Guy From Sugar Ray.

Do you think Ricardo Montalban is an Objectivist? You go back and watch some of that *Fantasy Island* shit and let me know. Notice how he's always *Mister* Roark? Like his given/Christian name is never given?

You bet your ass A is A, mofo.

the freemans

STACEY LEVINE

To begin with, we were far from the sea. My apartment door of soft aluminum never had the opportunity to hold back the sea.

My once-beautiful step brother had drowned, it seemed. There, standing on the porch, looking out: his new wife.

He stood next to her. The Freemans were a family now, the ludicrous metier of which nearly drowned me too.

They were a complex family and they could not relax. The new wife ravened for more, wanted to be crammed with prosperity and more so each year, sought to enthrall all comers with the velocity of her taste, her house, her son's forthcoming fame. Inexplicably, step brother joined her.

They were very nearly wealthy. Their stomachs were sore. They drove through Missouri, Iowa, Kansas, expanding their businesses; they did not look back. They wanted all the pastel drops in the world, all the granite countertops, linen, vehicles, foreign maids. They wanted piano lessons and horses without having to take care of horses and magic shows and boats and French spices and brand name sexual climaxes and all other people must be surpassed; this was the Freemans, and they would never stop.

It was an odd time in my life. Night, the arena for sleep, occurred with startling frequency: every few hours. When I woke, a beetlike scent hung in the air like a pheromone and between coughs I flattened my joints in the sheets, imagining assortments of dramatic sufferings.

Step brother was lost to me. Whereas once he had been a humid, fascinating being capable of comparing insect sex to the manufacture of silver, he was now merely a snob. His luminous half-precepts and lovely skin: disappeared. The new wife removed the flux from his wide eyes and the frequency of his gaze grew feeble. From my bereft state and buried sexual loss I emerged gaudy and cross, wearing moss covered sandals, slagging through sand.

Not long before, he and I had consoled one another frequently at sunrise. In a half-finished basement, we practiced Gung Fu together in resolute silence.

In the second season of their marriage the rain was stoic and in my distress I believed the wife had altered step brother's chemistry and turned his veins sclerotic and green. Without a doubt he had changed. Striding to his vehicle each morning, he waved at me fatuously, failing to see my apartment with its long corrugated kitchen and tiny window pasted with newsprint. Behind him rose his new three-story home, its innards hushed as velour, enveloping the soft multitudes of his errors.

Before, in the sparkling mud of our neighborhoods, he had flown to our hiding-place with thin calcareous limbs and faced me exclusively. His words fragmented around my ears and intoxicated me insofar as they were chaste and attempted to suppress what we both know. He refused to follow the family's demands; with his pendulous hair and gauzy palms he belonged nowhere.

Perhaps step brother merely became who he really is. It is true that in fits of nouveau riche ascension—the buying of businesses, the acquisition of a caged finch—he changed, then he and his wife changed again. The ease with which he undertook these changes revealed desires which previously he had concealed. The sequelae of his treachery went far beyond his lies and sudden egregious moustache. Perfunctorily, violently, step brother had affixed himself to the world. My disturbance grew as I recalled how, in the sand, he and I had tried to push the world away while bending to one another's gentleness.

His new desire to please others melded with a vile, bland sexuality and he took his wife from weakness, I alone knew. Neighbors and family clamored to him, swaying vegetally as if suspended in an oily extract of social convention and indeed, in a sense, he was free. I watched this repugnant transformation. Yet the precise nature of his former beauty still exists, at once real and impossible.

His profile being the sidereal light I still saw. It was the second year and I watched the Freemans always now. In the afternoon I stood at my table, working out cardboard puzzles, screaming at father over the phone for his insolence, his inability to swallow medicine; puzzle pieces dropped from my hands. Looking up, I saw into the Freemans' picture window where the new wife drank down a heinous frothy white drink. It is true that my vehemence toward her was ancient and that I might have attempted to suppress my temptation to follow the tradition of rivalry. But such an act would have been useless. Instead, I pursued an active distaste for her that gave me dull satisfaction.

Certainly the new wife was a creature who had, for example in high school, cried in order to manipulate her teachers and deserved my continued derision for this behavior because she had not changed. Now she generally starved herself, emitting an odor of wet cement and rapacity.

She had no sense of the scheming harlotish mystery of him.

Certainly I was a creature who could not feel pulses of love, not in the way others did. Admittedly instead I barred all people, though the act of predation held a purity for me that was piercing; thus often I found myself recalling step brother's hydrated scent and hummocky arms, his shorts which had been the grindingly beautiful color of blue. His silty averted eyes.

I had no intention of changing and exhaustion in me grew. It was nearly the third year, summer, a morning, and I virtually destroyed my apartment in search of a cup of tepid tea. The new wife had purchased several tiny sun dresses and this worked to addle me. Across the length of the day, I prepared a hot, thick, blindingly white soup and attempted to be calm. Through the window, I stared at the her and her child, who was now virtually grown, his body sleek as a capsule, containing a quiet air of entitlement. The boy chewed languorously on a drinking straw, then, sauntering to his new car, tore away, heading directly into the world to drink down its bylaws and customs as if they were distinctly unpoison.

*

Sliding my hands, I clear the table, unwell at the thought of the forthcoming family gathering now underway, its purpose to celebrate the Freemans' newest business breakthrough. At my shrunken doorway, Father appears in a dark wrinkled suit, gruffly beckoning. Voices of relatives mingle in velvet chords that tighten above a table loaded with glinting, unguent-like patés which absorb the heat of the sun. Unable to eat vegetable matter, I move away from the table, noticing among numerous tiny female cousins, a tall galutish one who, in fits of abnegation, tears herself from the group nucleus and stands below the high tension wires in anger: this is myself.

Step brother stands a few paces off in his aviator glasses and cheap muslinoid pants, holding, absurdly, a towel. Stepping near, I begin an exchange of banter; he gives a friendly shove. I return the shove and so on. Further shoves arise, mock slaps to the neck, his neck, his immense eyelashes, drumlike temple; I take his fingers and rattle them wildly as he ducks, feigning helplessness. But we both know that step brother has emerged into power, and its sources are, one, his bankrupt personality, and, two his obscene desire to eat, to lick up the world with his desecrated bloodied tongue.

I watch him return to the patio, change into tony swimming gear, my eye fixing upon the striae that run along his hips, revealing that, pleasingly, he has gained weight. He removes his wallet and hands it to Father, who stands by with a grin. Undeniably, Brother has always been in favor.

I go to him, lean back, kick his massive pelt; I tumble into him with jets of slaps and shoves sliding over his naked legs, my throat straining as ladies look askance, trying to shield the eyes of their children as I suddenly yell, still glancing at the striae, "I AM COMING" while Brother's laugh becomes as complex as a howl—

The family sways back. We wait. The sea at three miles away is even a kind of clock, a liquid timepiece waiting to assert its power to drown.

Silently, the family ignores everything, then turns away.

I raise my arm for another soft blow to Brother's jaw, then stop, drop: my decrepit titillation is gone.

The act of choosing a life is sad and requires that the discarded alternate lives atrophy in dirt and become hated.

*

Now, a game of horseshoes is underway in thc yard. It is key to remember that the coming winter will be a special one. Businesses will expand; futures will rise; and it remains that the Freemans, with their dark curvaceous hairstyles and hardy teeth, are much loved.

Pressing a hamsteak expertly to my mouth, I watch them remorselessly. Father shakes his wadded handkerchief; moist-snouted cousins discuss the brain chemistry of the poor.

My Brother always knew there was no where else to go but here.

The entire space of creation allows for happinesses of outsized proportions. Such is the joy of a fly who, streaking toward a lighted window, passes through effortlessly, without thought, into a territory of all.

This vast territory of the world gives countless children the opportunity to be born, to grow, to be cowed.

An ailanthus grows in a pot nearby and the pliant squeak of its leaves is tonic to me. The Freemans' son returns, his cheeks smiling and swelled with nutrition. Great sums of money are as evanescent as dance; the joy of a sister is untrammeled. Previously, I could not discern between such values as aberrance and strength, calamity and joy, insurrection and faithfulness, but now I am improved, fragrant with the succulence of hors d'oeuvres and dinner food. Who, after all, would destroy the Freemans and their home? Despite former troubles, despite all, I possess the active, glad heart of a relative, and looking to the Freemans, I salute them.

almost plum

PAULA COOMER

There ain't too many things I like more than a good pair of cowboy boots. Unless it's a nice swatch of leather, all sewed up to a good cut Italian vest. Or one of those silk rodeo shirts with pearl snaps down the front. Yessir, that and a set of Levi's will do my ass fine for a Friday night. You might say somebody like me could catch aholt of just about any kinda doin's in a get-up like that. Might even not find it tough to imagine how in a place like Moscow, Idaho, somebody like me'd be apt to sidle up to a kid like Tim.

Spotted him sitting on a bar stool in a place called John's Alley, lookin' kind of fussy, fidgety, smokin' one Camel straight after another. I sat down and bought him a beer. It cost me the second one before he'd even square me in the eye. You could tell by looking at him that he was somewheres in between where he'd been and where he was going. Hell, if he knew anything at all he wouldn'ta been in a tree hugger joint like the Alley.

After the third beer, he started asking out of the ordinary questions. Peculiar stuff like, "Is this mascara too black? Is my eyeliner too bold?" He was wearing Levi's, too, tighter'n flint on a matchstick, and a shirt with the sleeves cut off, and his hair was greased back like glue.

I finally shook my head and looked at him and said, "Son, I think you ought to come with me."

He gave me this prissy look, flipped his hand like a phony faggot and said, "Whatever for?"

And I said, "Cause darlin', somethin's twirlin' loose in your young ass and I'm gonna find out what it is."

We got to my place and it took two more beers and a shot of whiskey, but he finally let fly. Said he was barely nineteen. And scared.

He'd just slid his kiddie backside into that bar with a fake ID and got his first blow job in the men's room from somebody named Mick. A dimestore miracle in itself. There was hardly room to wipe ass in that little crapper much less get it kissed. I just looked at him. There was something about him, you know? He had this way like he was a pipe about to burst. Like he needed somebody to put him on the right train so's he could make it to the next stop. Made me think of the way my Carl once was when he first got to Spokane.

Tim sat there half the night talking about bein' a star. Said he'd been looking at magazines and watching MTV and he wanted that kind of life for himself. Said he wanted the fancy clothes and fancy cars and people hangin' his poster on the wall. "You just can't see all those people livin' their lives like that without wanting it," he said. Ever once in a while he'd kind of drift off and stare into space like he was lookin' at what it was going to be like.

It just so happened that the next day was the first day of spring and the biggest drag show of the year in Spokane. I looked at Tim and told him, "Son, you are only nineteen years old and here you are standin' on the tail of your own comet." I told him, "You listen here to me what you're gonna do." Then I gave him one of my T-shirts to sleep in and put him to bed on the davenport.

The next day I made him ungrease his hair, and we went shopping at the Goodwill for somethin' sparkly. After that, we hit all the blue hair joints in Moscow and Pullman 'til we found a decent enough wig, and then the Bon Marché for make-up doin's. I spent the afternoon listenin' to Tim cursing god because he wasn't about to be no fuckin' drag queen, while I Naired his wimpy whiskers and pancaked his face and dolled his lips red. By five o'clock we were loaded and on our way to Spokane.

Queers in Spokane are pretty much like any place else. There's an order to things, if you know what I mean. Anybody new has got to pay their dues. But that Spokane crowd, they liked Tim right off the truck. After two hours of coachin' on the way up, he sashayed natural-like onto that stage in a full-length satin thing that laced up the back, and long black gloves and blonde wig, and I'm telling you, honey, he took everybody for a ride. He had Sarah Vaughn wailing in the background and he was arching and swaying and by the time he was done the whole damn place was on its feet. They were hootin' and hollerin' and before he got himself back to our table, a dozen sparkly-eyed boys offered to buy him a drink. He sat his round butt down looking like it was the whole globe he had in his back pocket.

If it wasn't for Carl, I'da probably had little Tim myself that night. I had made myself a runway. And Tim was smart enough to know I dealt the game and played it in his favor, and that he *owed* me first take. But it's predictable for somebody young like that to fall into easy places, and that is just what his marble ass did. Considering the situation, and me brokering his fate, so to speak, I had a right to take issue. But there's something about missing a window, you know what I mean? If a thing don't happen the time it don't happen, maybe it's best to not be. Point of fact, Carl was the reason I adopted that notion in the first place.

You see, Carl was, in most everybody's estimation, the hottest thing in Spokane. He was the last pretty boy to come through and stick. And he was still a pretty boy, even after five years riding the beam, and pretty much got whoever and whatever he wanted. I'd already been greasing Tim up with dope and gin on the drive to town, and I guess I hoped Carl wouldn't be there, because I knew Tim to be a trophy he'd set his sights on. And Tim wouldn't stand a chance against Carl.

Carl was in Tim's shoes once, and he was the first boy I could say I ever truly loved. We met Halloween night in 1991, at a drag house in Spokane where he was about to make his debut. I walked in and he was standing against the bar with his boot heel on the rail. He had this padlock pierced into his navel with a chain through it that ran clear around his neck. And faded blue jeans. And the best lookin' Italian leather jacket I'd ever seen. Goddamned son of a bitch was just standing there. And he saw me as clear as I saw him. It wouldn'ta taken much for me to walk off the face of the earth just for the way he looked. Then he went on stage.

He had the Spyro Gyra in the background and he was gyratin' to match it. He moved to the music like he and it were one in the same. Where his ass wasn't, his basket was, and there wasn't a soul in the place took a breath. Then somebody came out with one of those economy-sized candles, and Carl struck a match against his jeans. They dimmed the lights and flipped on a strobe and off came his jacket. Carl arched backward while the guy with the candle poured melted wax all over his belly and nipples. When he stood up and started rubbin' his own fingers in it, half the place came.

After it was all over, Carl came looking for me. We danced 'til they closed us down, and then we went home to his place and spent the rest of the weekend ballin' and doin' lines. It was my usual thing to drive truck for Buell out of St. Maries, but I didn't go in on Monday, or the next, and after a while called in and told 'em where to send my paycheck. Being with Carl was like downtown Saturday night. A high ride on a Ferris wheel.

As they say, I don't know what happened. He always seemed to have something to piss and moan about. Said I dragged him down. Said he wasn't doing shows. Said he couldn't stand having somebody in his hair all the time. Said he thought it was weird I wanted him to go drag in the rack. Why don't you just go find yourself a girl, he said. It was my personal opinion that Carl's only real problem with me was the fact that he did as much coke as most people drink, but I guess when enough time goes by even honeysuckle withers on the vine. Finally one day I packed up and split. Hung around town for quite a while, thinkin' I'd give it a rest and try again. Then one night I popped into the club and saw Carl with some prissy little go-go boy and decided it was time to blow Spokane. My pickup broke down in Moscow, and that's where I stuck. A month later I ran into Tim.

I don't know who saw who first—Carl me, or me Carl, or Carl Tim. All I know is Tim finished his dance, Carl headed backstage, and I ended up leavin' the club alone. I admit I watched the Spokane paper for awhile, looking for I don't know what. A murder or an OD, I guess. But there was nothing. Two months later Tim showed up at my apartment broke, crying like a baby, telling me the same sad story as I've just told you. Only Carl let him down a little rougher. Told him he didn't know how to play good enough. Told him he was boring. I just handed him a joint and a shot of J.D. and said, "Darlin', men like Carl are useless as a buckle on a dishrag. Pull your head in out of the rain." I told my own story, and then I looked at him and said, "Ain't but one salve for a bunion like this. We're going to get ourselves some revenge."

Well, Tim took to that notion right away. We got up the next mornin' and bought ourselves some cans of whipped cream, a bag of frozen grapes, and three bottles of champagne. We picked up a cooler, threw everything on ice, and went back to my place to make ourselves righteous. Tim put on gold lamé hotpants and false eyelashes and almost nothing else and, honey, you could have cooked bouillabaisse on his belly. I had myself a pair of calf skin boots, a white satin rodeo shirt, my best jeans, and a ring on every finger. Once I threw my favorite black lingerie and a handful of neckties in a bag, we headed our asses out toward the truck.

I coached Tim all the way up on what to do. He wanted to go in with me real bad, wanted to see Carl's face when we showed up together, but I just said, "Darlin' if we both show up on Carl's step, neither one of us will get through the door." I told him it was time for him to learn a little thing called trust and to wait for me to make a sign with the window shade before he did a thing. I said, "Just look for me to close the blind and then you come on up do whatever you want to do to good old Carl."

He shut up for a while, then fussed about the rain, I reckon just to pass the time. "There ain't no risk of you dissolvin', darlin'," I told him. "Now why don't you think about letting the top part of your mouth keep company with the bottom part of it." One thing Tim could do good was pout.

When we got to the right place, I hauled everything up to the door and pushed the little button below Carl's name. It wasn't long before that sugar voice of his come on. "Carl, honey, let me in," I told him. I wasn't too much surprised when he did.

Carl was standing in his open doorway smiling as big as Texas when I got off the elevator. I pulled the black brassiere and garter belt out of the bag and he said, "Ooh, I love a vendetta." That's one thing I like about old Carl. He didn't even try to pretend not knowing what I was there about. For a minute it seemed like the old days.

"Honey, you are about to be fucked like fried potatoes on the hungriest morning of your life," I said. "Now get these things on and get me a line while I find us some glasses." As soon as I did, I walked myself across the carpet and into the bedroom.

Neither one of us wasted any time. I turned down the bedclothes and poured the champagne. He put on the brassiere and garter belt and dug out some nylons and high-heeled shoes. We did the line and I said, "Sugar, you are going to live to regret this night." Carl laid himself down on that bed and I spread out his hands and his feet and tied them up to the bedposts with the neckties. I took that can of whipped cream and sprayed it here and there. I poured champagne in his belly and drank that. Then I reached into the cooler for a frozen grape and popped it into my mouth.

I started it up first one thigh and then down another. I ran that thing up his armpits, around his neck and in between every finger 'til it thawed out. His flagpole was so high, you could have run a power line off of it. He was thrashing around and I just let him thrash there for a minute, then I got another grape, put it into my mouth, and passed it to him when I kissed him.

Carl didn't seem to have anything to complain about, so I got up to flash the blind at Tim and ran to the front door to wait for him to push the buzzer. By the time Tim did all that and got up the stairs and spent thirty seconds fussing about the rain, I could hear something funny coming from the bedroom. We both walked in there, of course, and when we did Carl looked like he was upset. I said, "Carl, honey, are you that pissed that Tim is here?"

Well. Carl didn't say a thing. He just laid there looking red in the face. In fact, he was looking real red in the face. Tim started wheezing about how Carl was dead, and I said, "He's not dead, honey, he's just horny." But Tim kept blubbering over and over about how I killed Carl, and I said, "Darlin', we ain't even got to the blow job yet." Then Carl made this noise like a cat hacking fur balls, and I decided I'd better take a closer look.

I didn't know what to think at first. There he was, flapping around with his dick in the air starting to look a little bit blue. I said, "Carl, honey, was it that good?" He kind of threw himself up in the air this time, as good as he could for the position he was in, and made that same noise again.

Tim said, "I think he's choking," and I looked at him and then I looked at Carl and well, all of a sudden I felt myself go loose in the gonads.

"He's choking, hell yes, he's choking, he's got a goddamned grape in his throat!" I screamed, and I fairly flew across the room and landed on top of him.

"Breathe, Carl, breathe!" I yelled. As you can imagine, I slammed my fists into his belly button as hard as I could. Carl was rolling his head back and forth, bucking like a juiced-up lab rat, and Tim jumped on the bed with us.

"That's not the way you do it!" Tim screamed in my ear and we both looked at each other at the same time and stared in our faces for a minute until both of us said, "UNTIE HIM!"

Tim took one side, and I took the other, and we undid the ties from the bedposts. Carl sprang himself out of bed and flung us out of his way and grabbed the chair from in front of his bureau drawers. There he was in black French unmentionables hanging himself across the back of that chair, and Tim was jumping around yelling, "Nine-one-one! Call nine-one-one!"

I said, "Tim, a 'possum ain't as big a fool as you are," and went to grab the phone myself.

"What do you mean there's a pile-up on I-90 tying up all the ambulances?" I screamed at the woman on the phone. "We've got a man choking to death in here!"

Tim was in the background yelling, "Hind-lick him! Hind-lick him!"

I hung up the phone and looked over at Carl, and he was looking pretty bad. "Carl, you are going to die," I said. The son of a bitch was going to die on us.

I don't know what came over me. I picked Carl's ass up with one arm and dragged Tim out by the armpit with the other. I ran us all three down the elevator, out the door, into the car, drove hell-bent, and then stormed us into the Deaconess. We stood there in front of that ER desk for ten, maybe fifteen seconds, Tim in his blonde wig and Almost Plum lipstick, me in my rodeo shirt, and Carl in his whipped cream and neckties.

"HE CAN'T BREATHE!" I yelled to everybody else. But they all just stood there staring like Granny at her picked-over Christmas goose.

"HE CAN'T BREATHE!" I said to the admissions clerk.

He took turns looking us all up and down with his John Lennon glasses and buttoned-down collar and said, "There's a waiting list."

I grabbed me a handful off the front of his shirt and pulled the end of his nose up so it could look at the end of mine and said, "Get this man some help or I'll get it for YOU."

That freak just looked at me and handed me the phone. He turned his pony-tailed, pussy head around, punched in some numbers and said, "Do it yourself."

I could hear myself breathing over the intercom. It's hard to say which was worse, not taking a pliers to the fag's teeth, or listening to Carl still trying to hack that grape out.

Instead, I talked into the receiver. "Would a doc please come to the ER Waiting Room? A doc to the ER Waiting Room? Oh, yeah, and make it STAT," I said. I will say I gave the boy my best down home smile after I spit on his phone.

A woman in a flowered uniform top and matching pink pants came bustin' through the ER doorway. "What the hell's going on, Lonnie," she yelled, and I thought to myself, I couldn't have hand-picked a better name for that homophobe.

Lonnie pointed her in our direction. "Sir," she said, "what seems to be the problem?"

Carl was still trying to hack up fur balls, and I didn't think that required one bit of explanation. Tim must have thought it did though, cause he said, "Carl's got a grape in his throat."

She said, "So, what's the emergency?"

Since I didn't see any point in standing around making small talk, I pushed the woman off to the side and dragged Tim and Carl into the ER. I guess that nine-one-one operator wasn't lyin' because the place was full of bloody people on gurneys with IV bags hanging over them and folks with stethoscopes around their necks yelling and throwing things. Metal was clashing and the paramedic guys were sitting behind the counter with their heads low over cups of coffee. The whole damn place smelled like swabby little squares of alcohol. It took about one second for everybody to notice us. A woman with short, dark hair and a hospital ID tag with her picture on it that said Marty Whitworth, M.D., walked over and said, "If you've got something stuck where you can't get it out, you'll have to wait in the Waiting Room with all the other citizens."

"Carl's got a grape in his throat," Tim said. Marty Whitworth stood there looking at Tim like he was the wrong kind of filling in her box of chocolates.

Next thing I know this big black nurse with dreadlocks came over and grabbed Carl from behind and started squeezing him around the middle. It didn't take but two or three shoves and that grape popped right out and rolled off and landed under a big red metal cart. First Carl sucked in air. Then he said, "Oh no." And then he puked all over Dr. Whitworth's brown suede Birkenstock shoes.

"Get his vital signs, and get them out of here," she told Nurse Dreadlocks. The woman I shoved against the ER door was asking about making a chart, and Dr. Whitworth said, "The less I have to remind me of this day the better."

So, Dreadlocks took Carl's blood pressure, gave him a pair of scrubs to put on, and said, "Bring 'em back when you can." He was real friendly, walked us out to the double doors and said, "There's only mostly rednecks working at Deaconess." I knew what he meant, and we all shook hands, and then he went back into work.

When we got outside it was getting dark already, and Carl said, "Let's go do a line."

It didn't take any more than that to get me interested, and Tim said, "Six of one half a dozen of the other," trying to sound suave.

We all got into the truck, drove back to Carl's, and sat up all night watching TV, drinking champagne, and snortin' coke. There's something about almost dying that makes you want to sit a spell, you know what I mean?

When the sun showed up, I figured it was time we was getting back to Moscow. Carl showed off in the brassiere and garter one more time, and Tim begged him to take him back. "It's way past your bedtime, kid," Carl told him, but I could see he still had something for that boy.

Me, well, I just held out my hand and Carl took it, then he grabbed me and said, "This is just another milestone, my friend, just another milestone."

Tim does the circuit now. Spokane, Seattle, Boise, Portland, and once in a while he'll pay us all a treat and drop in for the shows in Moscow. He's long since let go of that tail, darlin'. He *knows* he's a star. And Carl really is dead. He got himself a brain infection from using somebody else's mascara. The last thing he said on the day he died was, "It was more fun choking on a grape." Every time Tim is in town, we run up to take flowers to the grave. He always waits in the car while I go first. Says it's my unspoken right. And then I wait for him to do the same.

We don't talk much, driving back, unless it's raining porpoises, which was Carl's way of saying hell of a rain. Those times, Tim rolls down the window, sticks his fool arm out and says, "Wonder how it feels to be rain." I just shake my head and keep on driving, trying not to think about what I want to say.

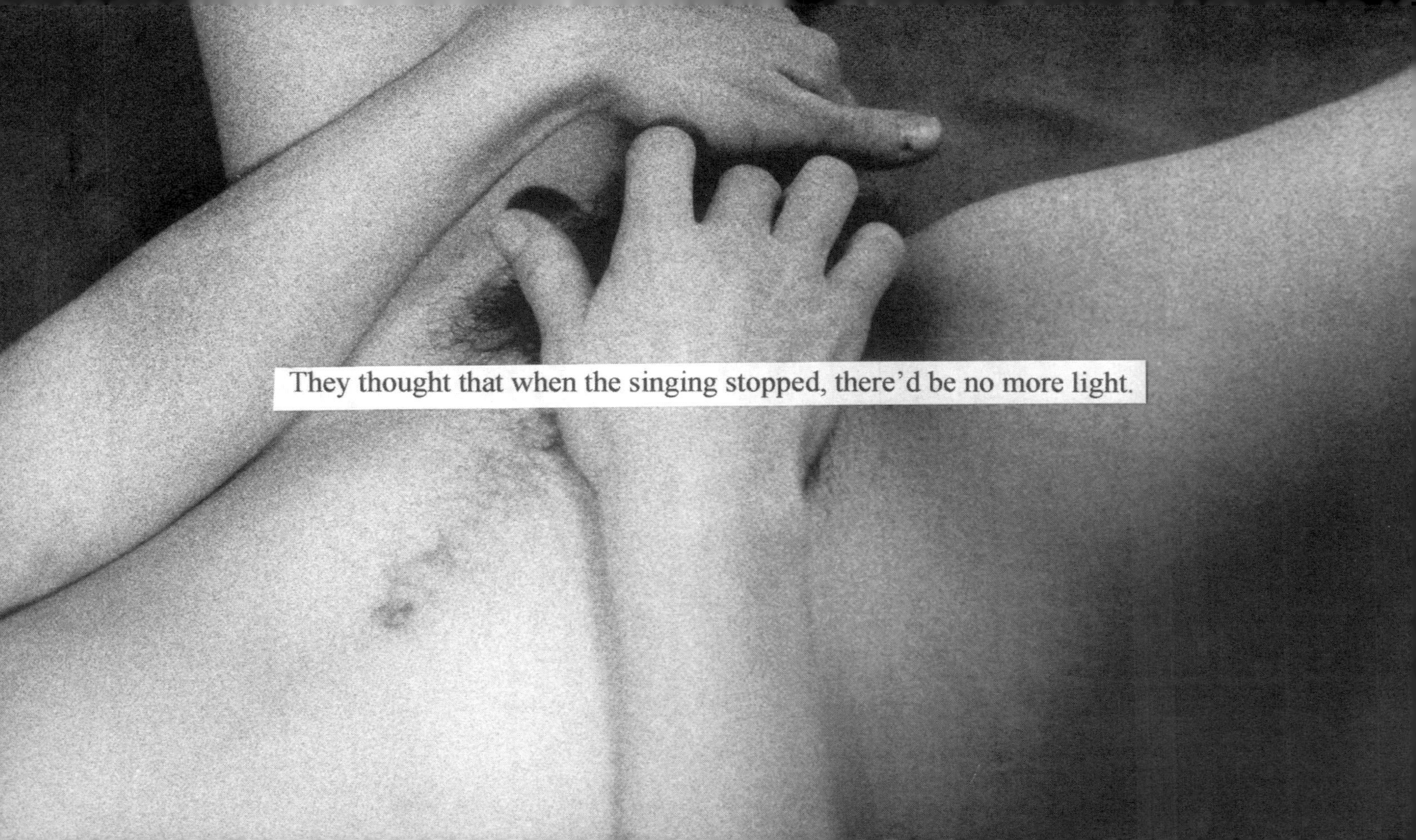
They thought that when the singing stopped, there'd be no more light.

You do what you have to do, he said, if you want to live.

from reduction

VIRGINIA PATERSON

Slice

Round, shiny. There's juice in there. Ready to burst. You have ripened to your fullest potential. I know you will taste good. Look at your size! Skin waiting to be ripped open. You were made to be devoured. I want to bite. Gently. I grasp you in my palm and dig my nails in right at the top. Juice squirts and stings my hangnails. Your outer layer is thick and firm, but right under that you're soft and pulpy. But the best part is right under that. The fruit of the fruit. Peel the thick skin back, peel all of it back to reveal the form underneath. Under your skin is where you taste sweet. Peel back the tough layers and strip away the stringy pulp until I've left you bare. Naked, the light comes through you, casting a glow on my sticky fingertips. I grasp you firmly in my palm and pry you open with my thumb. Sliding down, splitting you in half, your thin skin ripples from inside. Inside, your body is symmetry, each part needed for the whole and each part owning its own form. I steal away a slice of you, pulling at your pulpy hairs that are left. Squeeze your juice out and a trickle runs down my finger to rest on my knuckle. Your juice dries, leaving a crusty trail. I can see what you're made of. Each tiny envelope of juice within your thin opaque slip. Firm, cool, wet. I smell your tang, crisp mist of your tang lingering, filling my nose and the space between us. Stroke your skin, your juice comes out under my touch and makes you transparent. I lift you to my lips and lick you clean. Just a taste. I pull you back to enjoy this interlude. You fill my mouth with tart sweet and you slide across my tongue, drip all the way down, cooling on the way down. We've waited long enough. I bring you back to my lips and suck the juice and pulp out of your delicate skin. At first, you are firm and stretch through my lips. At last, you burst through the tip into the back of my throat, splashing millions of little pockets of your juice, scattering you all over my tongue. Your sweetness gurgles and drains down, down. Made to eat you, I was made to devour you. I chew your skin up, and hope your next slice is as sweet as this one as I eat my way through you.

Reparation

I like girls with little tits. Little sucklings. They're like candy. Little lemon drops I can fit in my mouth. Little tits have little nipples. Nipples I can flick on my tongue. No bitch with big tits has little nipples. All the big tittied chicks I've seen have enormous nipples. Scary nipples. Nipples the size of saucers. Nipples that turn into bullets when you lick them. No, I prefer tiny tits. Mosquito bite tits. Real tits. Not boobs. Boobs are sloppy. They flop all over. I've seen girls with big old boobs, and they slap them down on the table when they sit down. Sloppy. Boobs that big just get in the way. And I'd hate to see what those boobs look like in fifty years. Swinging in the wind, some bitch tripping over her boobs if she doesn't scoop them up in some enormous bra. Tight tits. That's what I like. Firm little kisses of tits. When those nipples get hard, that's all that's there. Hard nipples. That's all you need. None of this fatty breast lying around. Though, a small handful of tit is nice. Small tits that don't fall into a girl's armpits when I lay her down. No, I want those tits staring right back at me. Waiting for me to nibble on those cute tiny nipples. Waiting to get hard in my mouth and send her into ecstasy when she feels my cold wet teeth gnawing on her hard reddened nipples, pulsing with sharp pleasure. That's what I like. I like those girls with tits that they don't need a bra for. They can let those suckers just stick out, poking through their tank tops when there's a breeze. I like the underside of little tits too. When I work my hands up a chick's shirt, I don't want to feel her tits before I pass her rib cage. I want those little sucklings to be perched up, nipples aimed up, and stroke the curve of the underside. A little bulge, seamless. I like a woman with little tits because she's had to make up for being less endowed in other areas. They know they can't get anything with those insignificant little things, so they've got to make it known they've got other qualities worth checking out. And these girls can fuck like no one's business. That's all big boobs are good for. A fuck. Slap those huge mothers together and slide a big old prick between them. She's worked so hard to lug those monsters around, she's sure to be sweaty and ready, so stick it in there. Otherwise they just get in the way. Have to do that shit from behind because those boobs just get in the way. Yeah, I like little tits because it's not the first thing you notice on a chick. Big breasted women, you cant help but notice that right off when they approach you. And since the first thought that pops into your mind is their enormous boobs, you can't help but let that influence the rest of your conversation with her. Little tittied women are much easier to talk to. You don't have those tits getting in the way. Big breasted women with their huge nipples are scary. How can a god create such a thing? Something so unnecessary? Something so inhibiting? Something so grossly disproportional? Something that just gets in the way?

faust/faustus: a duet for devils, a performance

LEON JOHNSON

FAUST: Christopher Biddle
FAUSTUS: Leon Johnson

This performance project seeks to construct an interpretation of the development and manifestation of the HIV-resistant ccr5-delta 32 gene. This mutant gene appears in Europe, approximately 700 years ago, amongst Caucasian Europeans in the midst of the catastrophic Bubonic plague of the 14th century. Using textual excerpts from a range of Elizabethan texts and two versions of the Faust legend, Christopher Marlowe's *Tragical History of Doctor Faustus* and Johann Wolfgang von Goethe's *Faust,* a dialogue is created that examines the curative, persistent power of desire in alliance with the determined cellular trajectory of survival and continuity. With the knowledge of regenerative forces afoot, Faust and Faustus defy damnation and confirm their faith in a transcendent future determined by the utopian instincts of the genetic bodymachine. This presentation features a company of five performers, vocal compositions by Capra J'neva, video projection and an ambient score composed by Jeffrey Stolet.

Photography by JODY AKE
Video Images by MARTIN CAULLEY/CHRISTOPHER BIDDLE/WILL PETTIT
Faust Ring by JAI ROBERTS
Produced by CREATIVE MATERIAL GROUP

FAUSTUS:
I ASK YOU

[resolve me of all ambiguities]
look... am I in my text
or am I out?

FAUST:

NOW THAT I LOOK ABOUT I SEE
that you are indeed
O U T

FAUSTUS:

STRANGE

it is now that I know my soul
foul without and landlord
TO A BITTER GALL
. . . WITHIN

FAUST:

foulnesse is nothing more than a sign of

RIGOUR

FAUSTUS:

BE THOU

MY INERADICABLE

G H O S T

FAUST:

BE THOU

MY MELANCHOLY LIGHT

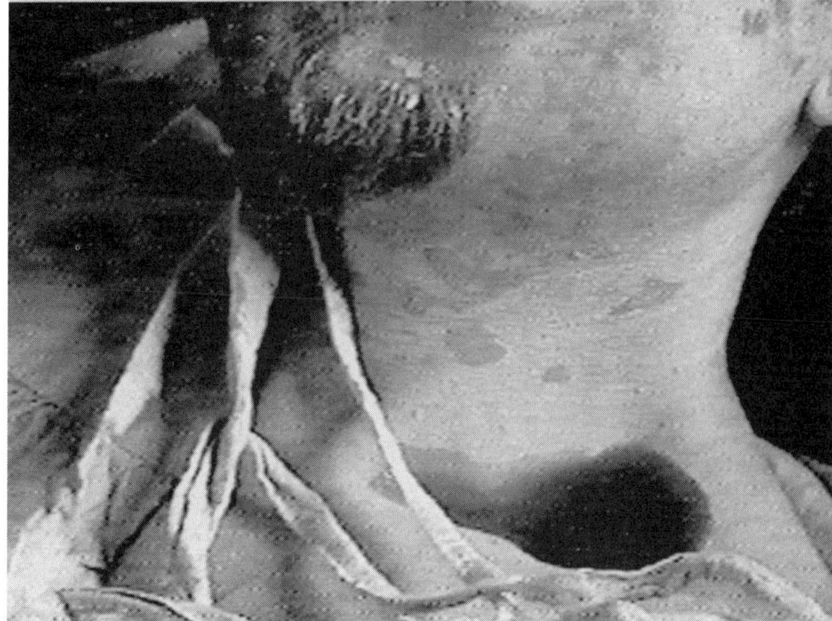

FAUSTUS:

STAY . . . LINGER AWHILE

[tis solitude I fear most now]

quiet proves nothing but prelude to

HORROR

FAUST:

when night comes and hath imprisoned our eye-sight

THEN OUR THOUGHTS ARE NOTHING

BUT TEXTS

to condemn us

FAUSTUS:

ARE WE TO HAVE NO LEISURE TO

WEEP?

FAUST:

O SOUL

to be changed to little water drops

AND FALL INTO THE OCEAN NEVER TO BE FOUND

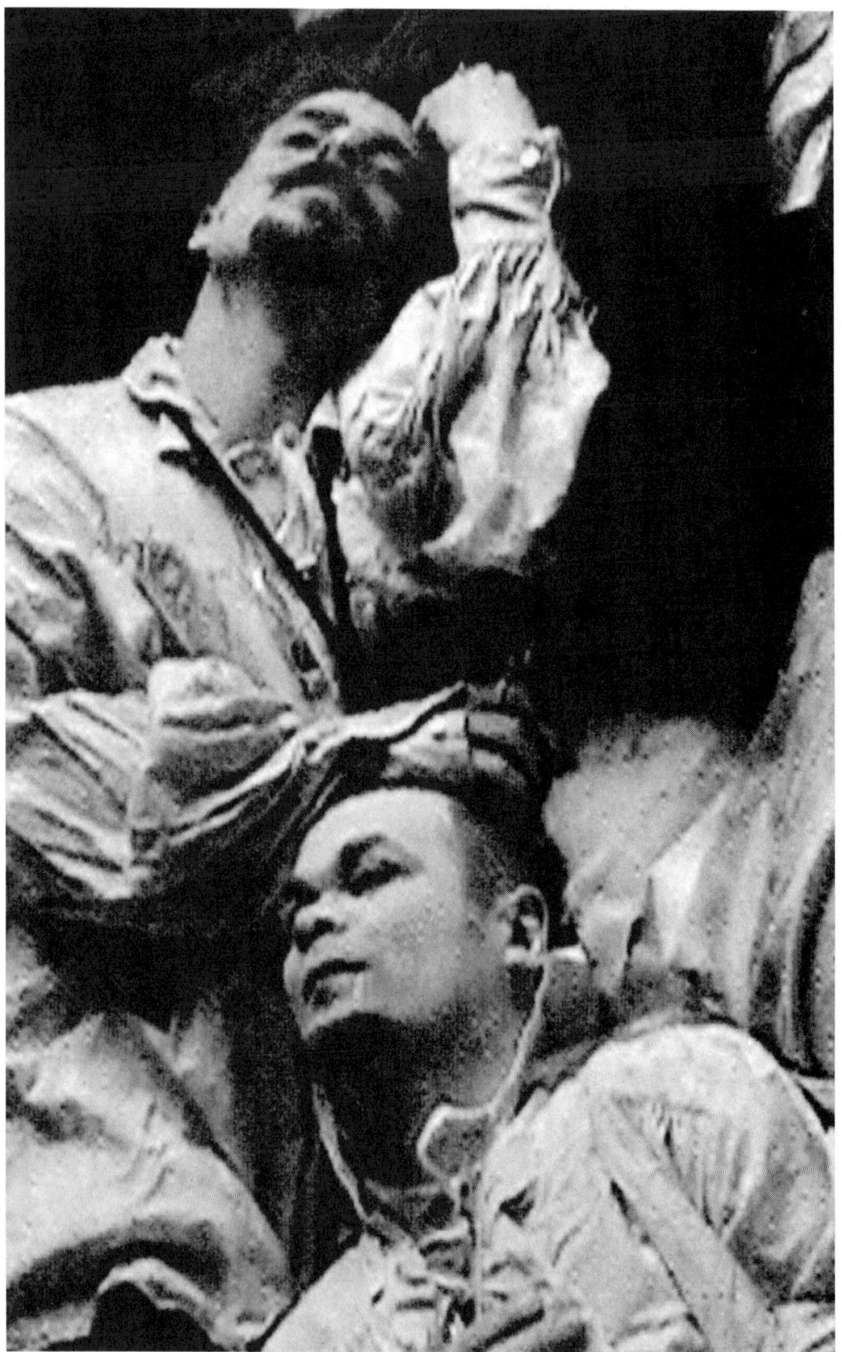

FAUSTUS:

I have a lover

c o l d

in Deptford

FAUST:

FAITH MY LOVE... WE HAVE INFINITE

WARM ENGINES

WITHIN US

the view: a diptych

DAVID SHIELDS

The windows looked out into the courtyard, but I usually pulled the shades. I've never been a big fan of the view.

*

"Aw . . . shit . . . I hate this . . . I hate this fucking life," the blind man said, startling everybody. "Fuck you, God."

nocturnal

STEVEN SHAVIRO

NOCTURNAL. "You were fond of me once . . . You always loved violence. You haven't changed, and you never will." Kurt (Christopher Lee) is dead and buried, but Navenka (Daliah Lavi) can't get his words or his body out of her mind. Mario Bava's 1963 gothic horror film, *The Whip and the Flesh*, revels in the poetry of this obsession. Kurt brandishes a riding crop, and savagely whips Navenka. His face appears in close-up, fixed in a haughty sneer. She lies prone, in reverse shot, writhing under the blows. Her nightgown is ripped to shreds, and lines of blood appear across her back. At first, all she can do is whimper and cry. But soon, her groans of pain turn into moans of sexual excitement. Her hatred of him is only a vehicle for her love. Kurt throws the whip aside; his expression changes. Now he is leaning over Navenka; he is about to kiss her. In extreme close-up, we see his face approaching. His mouth, avidly gaping wide, nearly fills the screen. This shot alone is far more violent and obscene than any whipping could be. Will Navenka be swallowed whole and utterly consumed? At the very last moment, the screen blacks out . . . These unearthly encounters can only take place at night. Night is the time when shapes shift, when forms and boundaries dissolve. There's no clear division between fact and hallucination, between life and death, between dread and desire. Navenka has killed Kurt, but still she finds him everywhere. He appears in the window, in the mirror, and silhouetted against the curtains. His sarcastic laughter echoes through the burial vault. He leaves behind filthy, mud-stained footprints to mark his passage. The doorknob creaks and turns, as he strives to enter. Such ghostly intimations drive nearly every scene. The action unfolds at a slow, hypnotic pace. Or rather, it doesn't unfold at all. In scene after scene, almost nothing happens. It's all disquietude and vague premonitions. Does that knocking sound herald Kurt's ghost? It turns out to be just a branch, banging against a window in the storm. It's hard to make anything out, anyway, in this blue-black murk, amidst all these shadows. The camera pans haltingly around a dark room, or tracks slowly down an empty corridor. It pauses, for a long time, on Navenka's face. But she is all in shadow, except for a band of light that crosses over her eyes. Suddenly she hears a sound; startled, she leans forward. Now her whole face is bathed in the light. The camera zooms in, capturing her features still more closely. She cries out and withdraws into the darkness. For its part, the camera pulls back too. Such scenes leave us in suspension. We feel the burden of the seconds ticking by. There's nothing we can do, except wait. The film moves at a pace that is not our own. It's a time devoid of action and events, a time of empty anticipation. Bava's camera moves to the rhythm of this alien time, as it tracks the minutest ebbs and flows of passion. It abandons the actors, and executes an elegant arabesque all around the room. Or it disrupts the balance of shot and reverse shot with a series of fast, irregular zooms. Or it holds on to a close-up for an inordinately long time. The film's most beautiful sequences have almost no dialogue, feature no dramatic twists, and exhibit no acting to speak of. They are purely atmospheric effects, conjured out of fluid camera movements, abrupt cuts, and subtle variations of light. But they are all the more intense for being so nearly impalpable. They tremble at the very limits of perception. They intimate passions too subtle to be detected, or too violent to suffer the light of day. They show us what can never be seen or touched or recounted directly. How else approach someone who is literally beside herself? Navenka doesn't possess a stable, coherent identity, for she herself is the one possessed. She feels Kurt's deathly otherness in her very bones. He is closer to her than she is to herself. His mere presence is a violence, a sundering. How could she not both love him and hate him, in equal measure, all at once? In the last scene of the film, she embraces Kurt passionately, murmuring to him of her endless love. At the same time she raises a dagger, poised to stab him in the back. It is only now, for the first time in the whole film, that we see things from an 'objective' point of view. Kurt, we discover, is not really there; Navenka is embracing empty air. It's the perfect emblem of her dilemma, stranded as she is between hatred and desire, between self and other, between pleasure and pain. Navenka thrusts with the dagger, aiming to kill Kurt again, and only succeeds in piercing her own breast.

Can you feel that, he asked.

strategies in the overexposure of a well-lit space

LANCE OLSEN
Images by ANDI OLSEN

37. THE DISCOVERY: CHANNEL

Kerwin Penumbro, who's taking his birthday off from his job designing and manufacturing certain popular body organs (a greasy heart still breathing in a madman's fist is a perennial favorite, though you should never underestimate the power of a bluish-white intestines wrapped on a surprised housewife's fire poker) at the small Japanese-owned special effects house, Goo & Pwin-Ti, just off Pioneer Square in Seattle, is expecting maybe a beige sweater with maroon stripes, or one of those Timex watches that lets you know the hour in Australia and Greenland simultaneously and is water-resistant down to a hundred meters, from his live-in girlfriend, Syndi Shogunn, who Ker met four years ago in front of the remainders bin at that just-slightly-kinked record store a block over, The Vinyl Fetish (Ker looking for the esoteric compilation on Air Pyrate Muzzik containing every pertinent Beatles song played backwards, *Re:Volver*; while Syndi, a secretary over at the local police station, ferreted for a disc housing themes to all those really great action-adventures-with-even-a-vague-connection-to-law-enforcement on the tube from the late sixties and early seventies to enhance her workplace ambiance, those golden years that brought you *I Spy, Mannix, Mission Impossible, The Man From U.N.C.L.E., The F.B.I., Batman, The Fugitive* . . . a-and even those truly warped masterpieces like *The Prisoner,* if you stretched your operational definitions a little . . . Syndi able to just go on and on about such things), but no way the knock on their apartment door this Thursday morning, Syndi away at the office, coffee spiking the air . . . not the May sun in Ker's rattled eyes . . . and certainly not the two men in khaki shirts and khaki pants and five o'clock stubble at maybe nine o'clock in the a.m. standing next to the neat cardboard box nearly five feet tall and four feet wide, saying: "Mr. Penumbro? We got your tv here . . ."

21. IMMORTALITY: STEALTH

A-and not your standard tv, either. Uh-uh. *This* baby is *humongous* and looks like it's been designed in a wind tunnel. It's made out of smooth black plastic and has lots of curves everywhere and Kerwin could under the right circumstances imagine it flying.

Plus it's one of the first HDTV models, the renowned Mitsubishi Stealth.

Plus it comes with one of those incredible mini-satellite deals you hook up outside your window and get like a bazillion channels on.

Kerwin Penumbro falls in love with Syndi Shogunn all over again.

While he's doing so, the delivery people search for the optimum viewing area, 7.4 feet to 13.6 feet from the screen, hook up the cable, adjust the tuning mode to AUTO position, flick the STEREO/MONO switch to STEREO, toy with the convergence panel, the quick-view, the remote.

Instead of breakfast, Ker sits in his bean-bag chair in the middle of the living room like a king in his bamboo throne on a South Pacific island (he's wearing only his grayish jockey shorts, which he knows as well as anyone should really undergo a good washing about now, but, hey . . .) and studies his owner's manual.

Instead of the nap he planned on taking sometime before noon, he makes himself this monstrous bologna birthday sandwich with lettuce, tomatoes, pickles, a wedge of onion, mustard, and this serious dollop of mayo (the expiration date on the jar barely noticeably out of fashion) on top of which he sprinkles cashews and what's left of his jelly-bean stash, tears open a bag of O'Boise potato chips, and flips the top of a Bud, collapses in his threadbare bean-bag chair 8.3 feet from the black monolith, squirms toward comfort, and clicks the ON button the femtosecond the delivery people nod, shrug, and close the door behind them.

Clicks the OFF button.

Stands, trots into the bedroom, rifles through his sock drawer, finds his last Baby Ruth, shnorks it for an improved disposition on the way back to the living room, squirms into his bean-bag chair like John Glenn into Friendship 7, clicks the ON button.

Clicks the OFF button.

Stands, trots into the bathroom, thumbs down the front of his Fruit of the Looms, relaxes his urethra, stares at the high-gloss ceiling (across which scrolls a single ant) while listening with pride to the vigorous plashing below, wriggles himself dry, pops the front of his Fruit of the Looms into place, whistling without really realizing he's whistling (the reverse version of "Strawberry Fields," doncha know), feels the sugar from the Baby Ruth beginning to itch the glassy horizon of his brain, trots back to the living room, squirms into this bean-bag chair, chomps into his sandwich, clicks the ON button.

Clicks the OFF button.

Stands, trots into the bedroom, throws on a pair of jeans and sneakers and a Sick Poppies t-shirt (this black woodcut of a sleeping head, python-long tongue lolling out and curling below like a garden hose, on a white background), trots into the kitchen, searches the top drawer beside the stove for his keys, grabs his black denim jacket in whose pocket he knows resides every penny he possesses for the remainder of the month (more than two weeks to go . . . a-and how did *that* happen?), jogs onto the porch, down the external wooden staircase, down the block to the 7-Eleven where he purchases a pint of Cherry Garcia, his fave, from an underfed chestnut-colored man without a thumb on his left hand . . .

Jogs up the block, up the external wooden staircase, onto the porch, into the kitchen, down the hall, back to the kitchen where he picks up a spoon and deposits said keys and jacket, down the hall again, into the living room, into the bean-bag chair, and, panting, clicks the ON button once more . . .

5. PRIME: TIME: LIVE

Kerwin Penumbro experiences his consciousness expand in a flood of sucrose-enhanced light.

141. DUCK & COVER

Nona Nova, hospital nurse, has battled illness on the eleven-to-seven shift. She has shocked a cardiac victim back from the brink of death; uncovered a plot by fiendish candy-striper Stephanie Stix to kill elderly patients; eased Dale Devin, young doctor, from his depression brought on by his wife Dolly's abscondence, a pending malpractice suit, and by his youngest son, little Donny Devin, dying in a freak fiery plane crash in the Andes (fog; tribal blow-gun competition); cheered up a child laced with tumors; unraveled the labyrinthian financial problems gnawing at Dustin Elwood, hospital head. Nona is thus understandably tired now. Her legs feel like hardening cement. Her head feels like twelve feet under a swimming pool. Her body feels old at twenty-seven. She stands in the restroom, staring forlornly in the mirror at the mulberry sleep-bruises gathered below her methylene-blue eyes, unzips her uniform, reveals her tight belly, almond-brown skin, pert breasts barely hidden under bra. She runs warm water in the sink. Splashes her face. Reaches for a handful of paper towels. When she looks in the mirror again another head floats behind hers: Rex Rory, flamboyant resident.

Nona Nova ducks and covers.

246. CARTOON GEL: HOMELESSNESS: LIGHT

Kerwin Penumbro claps in unabashed delight, forgetting he's holding the bologna sandwich, which pretty much disintegrates in his lap. Unfazed, he reconstructs it best he can and takes another bite and smacks in nirvanic satisfaction.

Because it's like living in a cartoon gel, the colors are so bright, the outlines so crisp.

Everything is animation rich.

A-and the sound . . . the sound is . . . Ker believes he feels spittle collecting along his busy lower lip.

Which totally undercuts the theory he developed as a philosophy major for his undergraduate honors thesis back at U.W., which states that imagination and desire continually outstrip technology . . . as in we're always waiting for the transistors to catch up with the synapses, always able to out-think the next mechanical or digital advance.

Nope.

He was wrong.

This appliance just about does it.

Though, true, nonetheless, that, weh-hell . . . look at computers.

If your basic car advanced at the same rate your basic computer did over the past two decades or whatnot, you'd be looking at a vehicle that'd travel at like five-hundred-thousand miles an hour, get a million miles to the gallon, and cost less than a down payment on a Stealth like this.

Which is simply to say things have gotten pretty . . . what.

Weird.

For instance, look at Ker looking at himself looking at the box, Ker thinks, looking. You'd imagine he was watching a really interesting sex arrangement through a one-way mirror when in fact he is watching this maybe awful soap opera which he simply can't turn away from.

Culture's first perceptual orifice, his theory goes, which is in fact someone else's theory, he's pretty sure, but, hey, was your no-frills cave door: primary purpose of allowing hominidal passage.

Culture's second, once we'd gotten beyond those load-bearing external walls, was, natch, the window: primary purpose of facilitating movement of light and air.

And but culture's third window?

Well, you're looking at it.

Or looking at Ker looking at himself look at it.

Except you don't look *out* through the third window, do you, reasons Ker. Can't. You look *in*. But the In you're looking at pretends it's an Out, which it sometimes is, sort of, if you think about it. Plus it's not so much that *you* look in or out as *it* looks in or out, kind of borrowing your eyes from you and every now and then forgetting to give them back. Plus what it does, honestly, is to bring stuff outside inside, such as it is, though the outside stuff pretends to be outside stuff when it's in fact inside stuff, as in produced and edited and so forth, and though it makes you feel you're always somewhere else when you're in truth always doing nothing much more than, like Ker here, feeling the spittle form on your lower lip while participating in the rampant overexposure of well-lit space, taking another bite of that really fabulous sandwich in a world without borders, because, if you stop and think about it, your home becomes someone else's home, doesn't it, your digital front door always being open, and not exactly yours, even while it's yours . . .

Which is to say nothing of stuff like e-mail a-and telephones a-and radios a-and . . .

Ker interrupts himself to wonder if he's heard, or only imagined he's heard, that there exists a model of the Mitsubishi Stealth that comes with a catheter for a prolonged viewing experience.

He'll have to order the catalog and check it out.

18. ROSES: TEACUP: REVOLVER

"You no good varmint!" the barrel-chested man in the white cowboy hat at the breakfast table is saying. Ker blinks. A tidy breakfast table. Three roses in a crystal vase. White tablecloth. Beflowered china. Tinkle of teacups. "You polecat!" he says. "You think you can plan my daddy's downfall and get away with it? You think you can sabotage his oil wells and mama and me'd sit still for it? Lickin' my boots is too good for you."

The barrel-chested man in the black cowboy hat smirks.

"An what you gonna do about it?" he asks.

"This!" the barrel-chested man in the white cowboy hat shouts, flipping an oily blue revolver into view.

211. AS SEEN ON TV

A-and faxes a-and beepers a-and cell phones a-and the World Wide Web a-and voice mail a-and answering machines a-and (in a sense, at any rate) VCRs a-and stereos a-and videocams a-and . . .

98. HE LEARNS HOW TO LOSE GRACEFULLY

Rope-and-log bridge wobbling over ravine.

Skydiver in red, white and blue jumpsuit. Lightning bolts on his helmet. Parachute on his back. Flawless teeth in his grin. He raises two fingers to his forehead in a flip salute to posterity, gingerly climbs over the cable, poises, arches his back, leaps toward the river threading below.

He plummets like a starfish.

You wait one one-thousand, two one-thousand, three.

He plummets like a car heading through the railing in an action adventure.

There is no white bouquet of chute, no slowing of momentum, no noise save the whipping of wind far above the tiny red, white and blue dot.

You watch him begin to flap his arms, a little at first, then harder and harder.

77. UNCLE BUDDY'S PHANTOM FUNHOUSE

Teenagers believe they are immortal, says this Rod-Serlingesque voice as the camera pans through the wooded night, which is clearly a Hollywood day seen through a special filter, fake car lights wobbling through fake pines on a lonely fake gravel road. *They believe nothing will ever happen to them. They live on their own psychic planet in a world where deodorant, hair style, jeans length, acoustic preference and mouthwash products matter deeply. They sleep profoundly, steadily, having all the dreams they should have . . . except these five teenagers on their way to this desolate farmhouse somewhere in upstate New York, who are under the false impression they are moving through a sexual and psychic rite of passage called a Wild Weekend at Uncle Buddy's Hunting Cabin that will involve alcohol, tobacco, and fire arms, not to mention certain acts of unprotected mildly illegal bodily combinations, will die tonight, and die horribly, one by one, mostly in nothing but their underwear, their breaths a hive of plaque and pre-gingivital fear at the hands of*

183. RUBBER WIG: CHILDBIRTH: HOMICIDE

"I's a killer," announces weeping Bobbie Joe Sue Alice Mary Bobson, who according to the ID at the bottom of the screen is a seamstress living in a trailer park in northwestern Florida.

Her hair reminds Kerwin of whipped cream in its hue and shape.

She will be buried in a piano case, it occurs to him, she's so fat.

"Share your pain with us," urges psychic healer Abbey Rode, whose hair reminds Kerwin of a red rubber wig. Abbey has that slack-muscled serious-yet-utterly-accepting face that only drugged children and talk-show psychic healers have. "We're here for you."

Abbey reaches out and pats Bobbie Joe Sue Alice Mary on the wrist.

Bobbie Joe Sue Alice Mary snorfles.

"My stepfather and his minister done abused my second cousin Pattie Bob Anne Frankie Patson when she was eleven."

"Sexually?"

"Snorfle snorfle."

Pan to empathetic audience faces riveted by the drama unfolding before them.

"What happened?"

"Done got her with child."

"Pregnant?"

"Snorfle."

"What happened next?"

"I didn't know none of this till last year, see. Only one night I's sittin' in my hot tub out back with my boyfriend Billy Ray Tom John, and Billy Ray Tom John? He turns to me and says somethin' real rude about my weight and all displacing the water and pretty much emptyin' the tub out, so I's feel liken to kill him. And then it all comes afloodin' back."

"The water?"

"The memories. All this red and purple. Scares me something awful. So I's of course calls the Psychic Healer Hotline."

"And one of my Hot Helpers talks to you . . ."

"Betty Earla Clarissa Lisa Simpson. Yep. And they knows somethin's real wrong right away, havin' second sight and all, so they's pass me on to you."

"Dhambala be thanked."

"Snorfle snorfle snorfle."

". . . ?"

"And then you and me, we come to meet and all and you redresses me to my former life and all, only afore we get there I take this what you call it detour and sees me afloatin' in my momma's womb . . . only I ain't alone."

"You're not?"

"I got me a brother I ain't never heard about. I's never had no brother before, see? I can tell he's my twin. He's in there with me. And then I start rememberin'."

". . . ?"

"He done raped me in my momma's womb. Every day. I'd just be, like, hangin' there and he'd come up and whump me and have his way with me and all. I's become my twin-brother fetus's sex slave. It's . . . snorfle snorfle . . . herbal."

"Herbal?"

"Turbal."

"Terrible. Yes. What did you do next?"

"I's takes it at fust. What's a baby-girl fetus gonna do? Only then, as my brain and amatomy develops some more and all, I's starts aplannin'. Float and watch. Float and watch. And I's wait till he's asleepin', see?"

". . . ?"

"It's night time, I knows, cuz I can hear my cousin-momma outside snorin' like a chainsaw gnashin' on a metal flag pole, and I real careful like just reach over and slip his umbilical cord round his neck, see? Never forgets the way his eyes sorta pop open, neither, all filled with surprise and hurt and all, and how he just starts aflippin' and aflappin' 'round in there like a hotcake on a griddle. Only thing is? Thing is, more he struggles, faster he dies."

"You murdered your own brother?"

Pan to shocked audience faces.

"We was born premature, him and me, only I done survived. My momma never told me about him, except I knowed. I'm a survivor. Been survivin' fer near a ten hunert years."

"Ten hundred . . ."

"That's who I is. Ever since I's fought the choppy Atlantic waters so me and my kin could discover Vinland."

"Vinland?"

"Vinland."

"As in . . ."

"That was me in my purvious life."

"The New World?"

"1000 A.D., give er take a month or two. Yup. Ol' Chris Columbus couldn't find a possum in his own britches . . ."

222. PLAY: SIN

Not long ago our culture believed play was a waste of time, an avuncular announcer's voice says, *a distraction from the truly important matters that kept a society whole and functioning. Some even regarded it as a punishable sin, the devil's work that chipped away at serious moral pursuits. But now most psychologists believe play is a necessary part of growing up. It helps children develop healthy attitudes and bodies. It paradoxically instills a sense of following rules and allows a chance for children to vent their excess energy. Recreational activities teach children to get along with others. The personality of a child grows as he or she learns new skills and develops confidence in sports—motor, sensory, or intellectual. In competitive games, he or she learns how to lose gracefully.*

59. THE GREAT WHEEL SPINS

The great wheel spins. The audience shouts. The game show host smiles confidently. Mabel Utta, sixty-two, from Dayton, Ohio, with a son in the Navy, jumps up and down, her fat chugging, and claps her tiny hands in glee.

1001. PRIME: TIME: LIVE

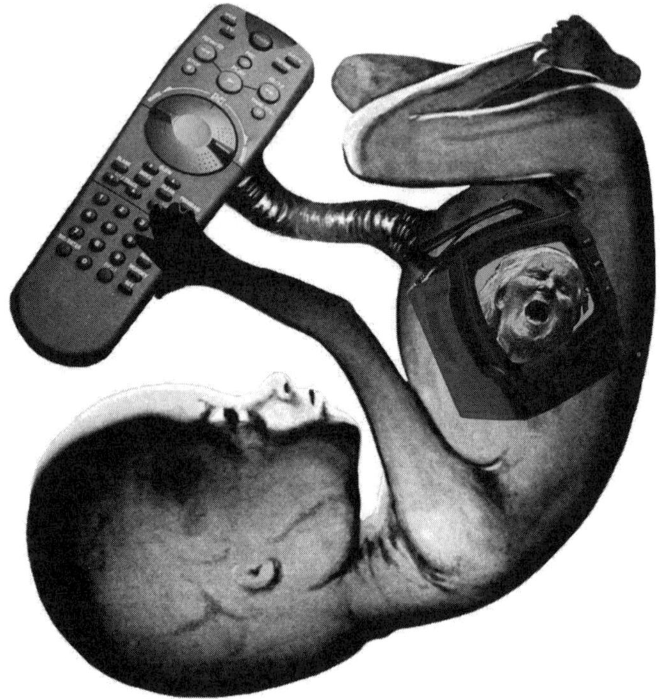

6. ART: CRIMES

Yeah, well, um . . . this is it? We startin? . . . What? Oh. My name is . . . my working name is Zondi. No. Just Zondi. No. Fuck the parental-naming thing. That's all about social control and shit. I was raised in Hackensack, New Jersey. I live on the Lower East Side now. Yeah. I'm a performance artist . . . What? Yeah. I knew it was my calling for like friggin' forever. When I was thirteen or something I saw this thing in this underground zine about this woman who performed surgery on herself and televised the operations around the world. I forget her name. She's dead now, I think. Liver transplant. Only I knew then I had what it took to be a performance artist . . . What? Oh, so no, the fucking bourgeois art establishment wouldn't accept me. That's the thing. That's how it all started. Fucking tight-assed fuckheads. I couldn't get in to even like a single art school. They said I didn't have no talent cuz I couldn't draw or paint or nothing. So I said fuck that. Those guys' conscienceness is like the size of a gnat's butt. I majored in communications. Which is what took me to Fairleigh Dickinson, right, which is this nest of cheesy reactionary fascists. They flunked me in math and social sciences and composition and a couple of other things I forget. So I said fuck that. I'd make it on my own. Which is what took me to the city, where I met Mongo . . . What? Right. Just Mongo. He's a good guy. He thinks and everything. He once studied with what's his face. And so he introduced me to the idea of AIDS . . . Arts In Denial & Shit . . . which it deals with art that denies it's art and all, you know, as in graphic design, only that gave me the idea for my magum okus . . . What? I'm nineteen . . . What? One-point-two million. Yeah. So anyways, I go to myself: fuck the commodrification of the arts on the fins of the millemmium. Fuck the fascist market. Fuck art dealers who wipe their asses with the masters like, you know, everybody. And, blam, right there in this nice café on the Lower East Side this cool post-strucuralistic concept of my magum okus hits me: NOT. Get it?. . . What? Right. So I decide I won't create a fucking thing for the rest of my life. See? *That's* my project. It's an act of negation deal, like. No paintings, no sculptures, no lithographs, no videos, no mobiles, no prints, no assemblages, no collages, no sketches, no nothing. See? I might do it with a punk rock band too. It's a statement . . . What? I don't know. What *you* think it means? . . . What? Sleep late, I guess. Listen to music. Last year I took up sailing . . . right after I joined that yacht club thing over on Long Island . . . which is pretty cool. I really like tv. Cartoons, mostly. *N.Y.P.D. Blue* has a very naturalistic perspective on our fascist society today which is pretty cool . . . What? Sure I got a VCR. Who doesn't? . . . What? Yeah, I guess. It's okay. I don't miss it. I don't miss it at all. Lately I've been thinking about taking up teaching. I figure maybe it's time to give something back . . .

13. SHE LEARNS HOW TO LOSE GRACEFULLY

She's already tired. Her legs feel like hardening cement. Her body feels old at nineteen. She stands in the back bedroom on the first floor of Uncle Buddy's Hunting Cabin and stares forlornly at herself in the mirror. Tom isn't the gentleman she had imagined. Or maybe Tim *is* the gentleman she had imagined. It's hard to tell. She unzips her jeans, skins them off, shrugs her Sick Poppies t-shirt over her head. She runs warm water in the shower. Her breasts beneath her lace bra. Reaches for the Ivory soap on the sink ledge. Her name is Melinda. Or maybe it's Glenda. Or Brenda. Ker either wasn't paying attention when it was mentioned or it wasn't mentioned in the first place. When Melinda or Glenda or Brenda looks in the steamy mirror again another head floats behind hers.

Zodiac Killer, homicidal maniac. Bright brown eyes. Flawless teeth in the mouth hole of his ski-mask.

He raises two fingers to his forehead in a flip salute to posterity.

The first teenager, wearing lace panties and bra, ducks and covers.

An ice pick glints in the shadows above her fourteen gallons of bleached-blond hair.

She opens her mouth to scream.

The ice pick descends.

The first teenager senses mortality.

201. THE DISCOVERY: CHANNEL

"Uh, hey. . ." Ker says, beer can pausing maybe two centimeters from his lips.

He leans forward.

Wasn't that . . . yeah . . . hey . . . wasn't that *Syndi's* face in the audience-reaction shot back there?

Okay, so maybe it took a couple of minutes to register, but fer shure it was, has to be . . . just after that what's-her-name, fat lady with the whipped-cream hair, admitted she whacked her own fraternal twin in flagrante utero.

Steady, boyo. Steady.

He leans back.

Lessee.

Okay, Take Two: there was this anorexic mom-type with green turtle-shell glasses next to a black rodential woman with simpatico tears in her eyes . . . a-and right behind them, bobbing just out of focus, was . . . Syndi . . . yeah, Syndi . . . Ker'd of course recognize her anywhere . . . long honey hair in a ponytail . . . wire-rimmed glasses . . . slightly puzzled brown eyes . . . almost like Ker wasn't the only one wondering why she was there . . .

Only . . . why *was* she there?

She's supposed to be at work today, right? Plus she's never mentioned the Psychic Healer Network. Plus that show was shot . . . where? New York, probably, or Chicago.

Cr*eeeeee*py.

Ker shudders.

Weh-hell . . . these things were always prerecorded, weren't they, bordering as they always did on a species of well-disguised infomercials, and, uh, Ker guesses it was just possible this was taped like four years and one day ago, twenty-four hours before he stepped into The Vinyl Fetish, or maybe seventy-two, or maybe three months, which isn't the point, is it, but nonetheless . . . maybe it represents just one of those little secrets lovers keep from one another, or . . . not so much secrets (Ker simply couldn't contemplate such a thing hanging between Syndi and him like one of his body organs on the drying hooks down at work) . . . as just, um, what . . . just unexplored psychological territory that would under the right circumstances become totally mapped.

Unless, it goes without saying . . . unless it *wasn't* Syndi, but one of those look-alikes you see all the time on the streets around town who you could swear was like Ellen DeGeneres or that woman from *Friends* or something, except wasn't.

Right?

With one hand Ker tips back the Bud for a long mind-clearing swig and with the other flips channels in reverse, descending the decision tree, trying to relocate that show . . . only the thing is . . . the thing is . . . he can't.

Okey-dokey. Not to worry, he thinks, starting, needless to say, to worry. Not to panic. He's been hopping around a lot, and hasn't a clue where exactly he's been.

It's all right.

No sweat.

A-and he hasn't been looking at the time . . . so for all he knows the show is already off the air, replaced by an infomercial about how to hit it rich by buying all these houses in Arizona or investing in Rogaine or something, o-or maybe another guest and host are on in the second segment (if indeed the fat woman and healer comprised the first), o-or maybe there's a commercial cycling and so he's in fact looking at the right channel but it feels like he's looking at the wrong one.

"Shit," Ker announces, clicking.

This horrendous green snot bubble balloons out some pig-snouted female kid's left nostril and the well-dressed woman across from her at the nice LA restaurant begins spontaneously kecking.

Click.

A woman with stelliform shoe-polish black hair's head derricks up and down in a man's naked lap.

Click.

Prosthetic surgery is painful, but it can powerfully renew our sense of involvement in the world. It's all a question of where you locate the information interface: how much you can stand to lop off, or just how far back you're willing to go . . .

Click.

A reddish-brown male *Cimex lectularius* (bedbug to you and me) in ghastly close-up stabs its beak into a female's abdomen, preparing to release its sperm into her wound and hence bloodstream.

Click.

Tribal drums and primitive wails blossom. Colors whirl. Black men in grass skirts and jangling brass earrings, bracelets, and necklaces dance wildly around a bonfire, shaking spears, lifting knees, hooting and jabbering at the nightspirits. Their earlobes hang to their jawbones. Scars funnel their cheeks. Only the whites of their eyes show. Ker believes they're real, but feels there's an equal chance he's just watching a rerun of *Gilligan's Island*. They leap and caper around a naked pale body tied to the ground, ready for sacrifice. Arms stretched out to the sides. Legs wide apart. The face alert, familiar . . . very familiar . . .

Click.

A-and it' . . . it's . . . OUTTA HERE!!!

111. AS SEEN ON TV

44. DUCK & COVER

"What you gonna do about it?" the barrel-chested man in the black cowboy hat asks.

Ker feels in familiar territory and settles back in his bean-bag chair.

"This!" the barrel-chested man in the white cowboy hat shouts, flipping an oily blue revolver into view.

"Good Lord God, *no!*" the mother in the white cowboy hat cries, trying to stand, crinkled and old.

The barrel-chested man in the black cowboy hat tries to duck and cover. But it's too late. The barrel-chested man in the white cowboy hat fires. China crashes. Crystal splinters. A chair cracks against the floor.

"*Uggggh!*" the mother in the white cowboy hat cries, fatally wounded.

111. AS SEEN ON TV

"Say what?" Ker says.

249. AS A SOAP OPERA

It is also worth mentioning that although egg consumption in the United States is one-half of what it was in 1945, there has not been a comparable decline in heart disease. Moreover, although the American Heart Association deems eggs hazardous, a diet without them can be equally hazardous. Not only do eggs have the most perfect protein components of any food, but they al

3. ▬▬▬▬

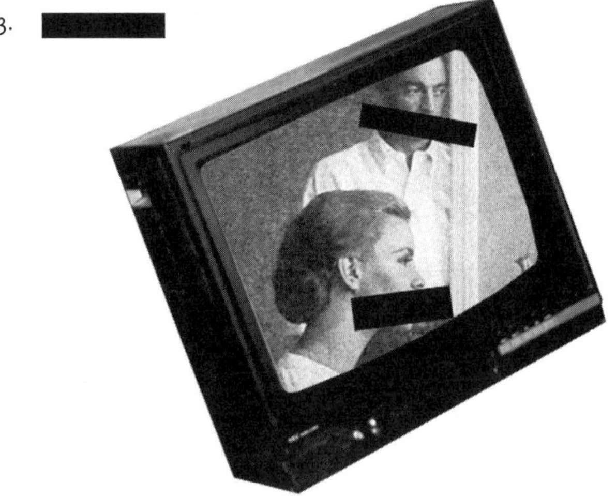

68. DUCK & COVER

A glistening black Porsche sizzes through what looks like downtown Dallas or downtown Miami late at night, screeching around corners, turboing through intersections. A Corvette jets down avenue after avenue, low slung, white, locked in overdrive. Scattered gunfire. Because of the rapid jump-cuts, it's unclear exactly who's chasing who. Closeup of Rex Rory behind the wheel of one of the cars (though which is unclear), perspiration sparkling on his face, fury in his eyes, hatred at mouth corners . . . most likely, given the context, not playing the flamboyant resident (though this obviously is open to debate and readjustment through viewing time) . . . followed by the closeup of that barrel-chested man in the black cowboy hat, sweat sparkling on his face, eyes wide with fear, nose now broken and swelling, who isn't, in fact, Ker is almost sure, the guy from the other show, though it's possible he is, in which case next week's episode is playing simultaneously with this week's, only on a different channel, or maybe the syndicated version of the show (whose name is on the tip of Ker's tongue) from let's say two years ago is cycling simultaneously with the so-far-non-syndicated version, only on a different channel. Ker in any case has the sense that he's missed too many pieces of the plot to understand very much. An excess of lines have been spoken without him there to hear. He might as well give up. Plus he has the feeling he's seen this one before . . . until, that is, the wedge-shaped spaceship appears, a glowing green delta over the city, and simply tremendous, as in the size of a hovering battleship, and it's busy shooting some sort of photon-torpedo-looking jobs at *both* cars, only the aliens inside are really bad aims and keep nuking wads of unsuspecting tourists who have no right to be standing on street corners at this time of night in this kind of iffy neighborhood anyway. Until, that is, the camera zips inside said ship, and Ker sees the two standard-issue cute human kids at the control panels, maybe twelve or thirteen years old, all agitated, trying to fly this thing and clearly pushing the wrong buttons by accident, and it dawns on Ker this whole business is really a comedy, the kids having crept aboard said craft probably built by dad in Utah or something and bumped the throttle without knowing it and now are on some kind of cartoonish joyride, ha ha . . . unless, uh-oh, Ker thinks, they aren't kids at all, but scary kids-appearing aliens, maybe pod-kids, and this ducks-in-a-barrel thing is their idea of a good time, and maybe they aren't on earth at all, but on their home planet, a-and this is simply their playground out back or in their cellar, a-and the guys in the cars and all the bystanders have been unknowingly kidnapped and transported here while they slept a-and still believe they're in Dallas or Miami, which from their perspective is being invaded, which is a possibility definitely worth considering, in which case it's really a horror film that's super intelligently conceived, though Ker kind of doubts it, but decides to go along with the flow anyway, since it'll make his viewing more palatable. Until one of the kids or pod-kids or whatever lifts a can of something apparently called a Zerp soft-drink and takes a chug followed by a wide satisfied smile, and the announcer, this French guy who sounds like he's on barbiturates, says something Ker can't understand, though he once back-packed through France for two weeks, and in college took two years of the stuff, and Ker realizes he's been inhabiting a commercial masquerading as a horror film masquerading as a comedy masquerading as an action adventure masquerading as a soap opera.

76. NEWS: BREAK

A blueblack fly alights on the eyebrow of a young black boy whose facial skin has shrunk and withered like

666. HOPE FLOATS

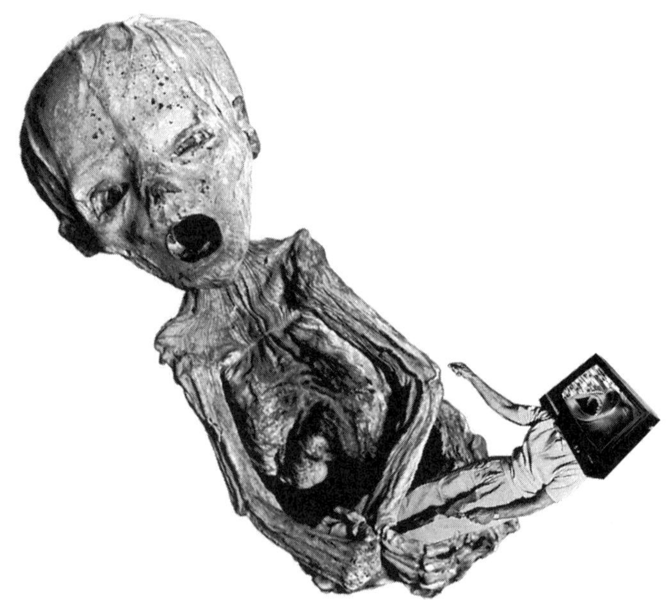

99. THE GREAT WHEEL SPINS

The great wheel spins, brilliant light fizzling like fireworks. The audience shouts insanely. The game show host smiles confidently. Bertha Marcella, fifty-eight, from What Cheer, Iowa, with a son in the Marines, jumps up and down, her fat chugging, and claps her tiny hands in glee.

Then a shadow crosses her face.

She feels the pang.

Feels the elephant sitting on her chest.

The lightning in her left arm.

Her face muscles slacken. Her hands drop to her sides. Her eyes look up at the ceiling in disbelief. Bertha opens her mouth, sticks out her tongue, and topples over backwards.

She is wearing, Ker notices, a Timex on her left wrist.

31. THE DISCOVERY: CHANNEL

A cartoon dustcloud churns across the cartoon desert under a cartoon sky that's eerily pink instead of blue.

It's Wile E. Coyote. He's wearing a pair of Acme rocket boots. And the Roadrunner is doing that thing the Roadrunner always does, just kind of gliding nonchalantly along on those whirling legs of his . . . cool, calm, dum-de-dum, with even this like semi-reptilian smirk carved into its beak.

Only something's wrong here.

Ker expects those rocket boots to blow up any second. Or, you know, a huge rock or cactus to zoom up out of the desertscape and slam the poor carnivore so hard he can't stop vibrating for the remainder of the episode. O-or maybe some other gadget he tried to use earlier in the skit (an anvil, say, or an Acme ICBM, or a turbo-powered car right out of the Jetsons' garage) to appear and burn his sorry ass to a crisp cinder.

Since, as Ker and every other philosophy major who's ever watched this show knows, Wile E. is none other than the animational embodiment of Sisyphus, and the Roadrunner his boulder, and the desert his hill, and the poor guy is just never going to win, it's so obvious it hurts. He's going to fall, explode, leap faithless into oblivion, squish, become existential flypaper for every bit of bad karma the uncaring universe can dish out. That's the given. But his dignity (oh, yeah, have no doubt about it, folks: that's *dignity* you're witnessing there) arises from the fact that he *knows* this and just keeps on going anyway, fuck the degenerate swine at Acme, you've got to *believe*.

Except . . . he's gaining ground, is the thing.

Wile E. Coyote's actually closing the gap. There goes another ten yards, and another five, and he's stretching both arms out in front of him, sort of leaning into the momentum as the exact same background cycles over and over again behind him, and the Roadrunner is actually looking over its shoulder, a little nervous now, that frozen smirk beginning to melt, and Wile E. reaches down to the control panel on his belt and hits OVERDRIVE.

Zoooooooooom!

And, *wham*, he's got him!

Yep.

Wile E. grabs the Roadrunner by the neck with one hand and turns off his rocket boots with the other and there they suddenly are, huffing in the silent desert, orange sun beginning to set behind them.

Holy fucking cow.

Only . . . hey . . . what's *that*?

They . . . *embrace*! Yeah, and if the truth be known there's nothing female about that big bird and . . . what the hell's *that* all about???

The Roadrunner slips Wile E. his tongue, and Wile E. reciprocates, a-and pretty soon it sort of inches up on Ker that the Roadrunner's just been playing hard to get all this time . . . yeah, that's it, the whole thing's been one big come-on . . . and now what you've got yourself here are two really randy cartoon characters, a-and . . . whoah . . . old Wile E.'s getting down on his paws and knees . . . a-and the Roadrunner's kind of shuffling up behind him . . . a-and, *argggggh*, that ain't no tongue, man, that ain't no beak . . . that's . . . that's . . . that's . . .

169. THE LOVEBOAT

Nona Nova, hospital nurse, stares forlornly at herself in the mirror, unzips her uniform, reveals her tight belly, bronze skin, pert breasts barely hidden under a lacy bra. She runs warm water in the sink. Splashes her face. Reaches for a handful of paper towels. When she looks in the mirror again another head floats behind hers: Rex Rory, flamboyant resident. Nona cracks a smile.

Rex steps into the women's restroom quickly and shuts the door behind him, flashes her a flawless grin.

They embrace.

"Oh god, how I've missed you!" Nona murmurs into his ear.

He squeezes.

"Yes, yes, yes!" he whispers.

They kiss.

She reaches for his belt. He reaches for her breasts. For her belly. For the astonishing curve of her spine.

"Hey, wait a second," he says, feeling that weird bulge in her panties. "What's this?"

33. DUCK & COVER

51. A PRICK

The male platypus possesses a hollow claw, or spur, on each hind leg. The spurs are connected with poison glands. The platypus pricks and poisons its enemies when it feels threatened.

9. PRIME: TIME: LIVE

There is no white bouquet of chute, no slowing of momentum, no sound save the whipping of wind far above the tiny red, white and blue dot.

You watch him flap his arms.

Watch him kick his legs.

Speed down, faster and faster. Shoot down. Hum down. Hurtle straight for the jagged rocks and shallow river below. The strong current. The icy water.

The twisted bodies of those who tried and failed before him.

188. ADDRESS AT VISION 31

"Uh-oh," Kerwin says, glancing down at the last bite of his sandwich pinched between his thumb and forefinger.

He isn't feeling so hot all of a sudden.

His stomach's queasy and his head's all . . . it's kind of like when you have the flu and the rest of the world looks like you're squinting through a layer of Saran Wrap someone's coiled around you.

He starts giving some serious thought to that mayonnaise.

It *did* taste sort of funny.

Sour, like.

He puts the last bite of his sandwich on the end-table next to his bean-bag chair and, weh-hell, just leaves it.

Plus he hasn't been paying attention to the time, but now the light in the room's changed for the unmistakably more somber, taken on a resolutely late-afternoon hue, unless obviously the sky has clouded up, in which case it could be any time of the day . . . only he senses Syndi should be here by now. The apartment should be full of her presence. He should be smelling dinner cooking. He should be listening to her tell him about her day as she tinkers in the kitchen.

Maybe it *wasn't* her on that show. . .

After all, the idea didn't even suggest itself until minutes later, did it, which only goes to prove how the mind isn't always what it's cracked up to be, you know?

Maybe Syndi has a twin sister . . . did he ever think of that?

O-or maybe not a twin so much as a sister who looks enough like her to be mistaken for her twin sister.

Only Syndi doesn't know because they were separated at birth.

O-or maybe it's possible, given the ultimately limited genetic resources on the planet, that someone shares enough of her cellular patterns that on a tv, across great distances, she could easily pass as Syndi.

It could happen, Kerwin thinks, reaching for his beer and then deciding against it.

Fer shure.

Why not?

3. OPEN HEART MESSAGE

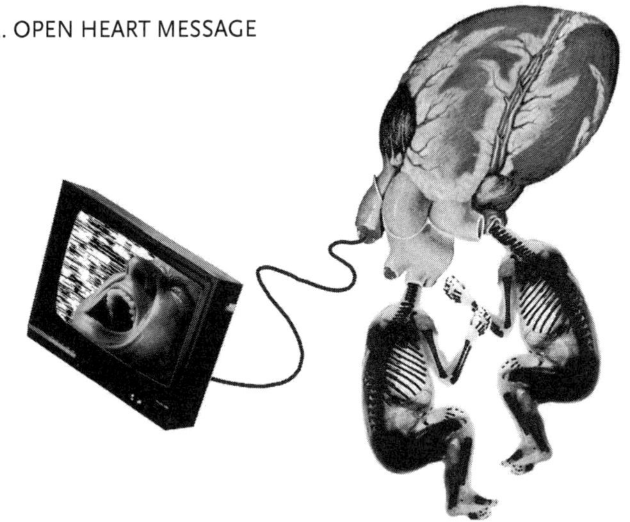

107. VINYL FETISH

Mildred Openheimer, sixty-three, from Onaway, Idaho, with a son in the Air Force, opens her mouth, sticks out her tongue, and topples over backwards. She hits the floor like a whale dropped from a 747.

Just at the moment the wheel stops spinning.

Just at the second its arrow points to JACKPOT.

Just at the instant sirens begin to shriek and buzzers to trill and alarms to rattle.

The game show host, Sam Slant, close-cropped graying beard and slicked-back hair, still smiling, looks down at Mildred, up at the camera, over at the other contestants.

"Um," he says.

Which leads Ker to assume he's watching a speedily goofed-up game show until the two detectives in black, one short and one tall, one chubby and one underfed, walk out on stage and it becomes clear this is the old game-show-within-a-police-show trope.

At which time Ker realizes Mildred is being played by Sandi Slam, the same young actress who plays Nona Nova, only she's all decked out in layers of foam to make her look huge and old, which impresses Ker a lot, from a professional point of view.

But not as much as the explanation that the short chubby detective with a head shaped vaguely like a hammer delivers, hardly moving his lips, as paramedics begin to work on poor Mildred whose mouth is opening and closing like a pithed frog's.

Mildred Openheimer, unhappily married to one Marvin Openheimer, and unhappily mothered to Murray, Mini, and Mimmi Openheimer, and feeling really alone way out there in Onaway, Idaho, became involved with the Internet as a way to meet people. She joined a number of chat groups. One of them, which she thought had to do with discussing old-time records, was called The Vinyl Fetish and was frequented by all manner of S&M types, one of whom went by the moniker Slowhand.

Mildred fell through the looking glass, discovering a world with him she never knew existed.

And she liked what she discovered.

So before long she took on the handle Black Widow, having very little appellative imagination left, given all that time in that little town, and off they went.

At first Mildred and Slowhand gabbed nightly in the chat space while Marvin stared at the tube just a couple of feet away, spinning all manner of increasingly sicko fantasies to basically pass the time . . . except then they gradually elided into e-mail correspondence, where suffice it to say the words *tit clamps, penis rings,* and *nice fucking slow strangulation* came up a whole bunch more frequently than in what you might conceptualize as conventional day-to-day friendly discourse.

One morning a month ago Mildred waited for Marvin and the kids to leave for work and school, respectively, packed a suitcase, and, without even scribbling an adios note, vamoosed, traveling via train to LA where Slowhand (aka one Ralph Schnorz, a five-o'clock-stubble-at-nine-in-the-morning kind of guy if ever there was one) was waiting.

They met at a hotel where Schnorz employed some of the ideas on Mildred they'd been discussing digitally, then went downtown where they got her on this game show, The Great Wheel Spins, and, seconds before she took the stage, fed her three prophylactics packed with heroin, each with a hairline tear in it, which ruptured the eyeblink she began jumping up and down, releasing enough diacetylmorphine into her system to kill something like eighteen elephants and maybe a lion and two or three water buffalo besides, executing the sadomasochistic double-suicide pact they'd been weaving for almost a year, which means . . .

"Hic, hic, hic," Sam Slant, game-show host, says, beginning to gag. "Hic, hic, hic."

He reaches up and with a flourish yanks off his beard and toupee, revealing, yep, the bald-headed pock-marked five-o'clock-shadowed features of none other than Ralph Schnorz, sadomasochistic killer, who has himself just bitten down on a cyanide capsule he bought on a recent trip to Tijuana, but not before ripping away his clip-on tie, popping the buttons down the front of his white Armani shirt, and dipping inside for one more yank on the biggest tit clamps you've ever seen, more like something you'd find on a worktable in a hobby shop than anything you'd ever expect to find on your average human body, at which point the *real* Sam Slant lurches up in the middle of the audience, burbling mostly to himself as *his* hit of heroin finishes its work, and topples face forward onto unsuspecting Mabel Utta, sixty-two, from Dayton, Ohio, with a son in the Navy, whose osteoporosed neck snaps instantly, actually detaching from her body in a geyser of blood and tumbling bowling-ball-like through the initially baffled and then increasingly horrified audience, sending blue-haired women right and left into immediate cardiac ricti, not to mention one of the lighting guys wearing khaki shirt and pants, one Billy Ray Tom John, recently arrived from Florida on the heels of a really ugly breakup with his really ugly girlfriend, her adipose tissue still giving him nightmares, who dies quickly and almost painlessly, but not before thumbing the switch that sends several tons of klieg lights hurtling down on the two detectives who duck and cover . . . but without much lasting success.

431. LOOKING GLASS GEYSER

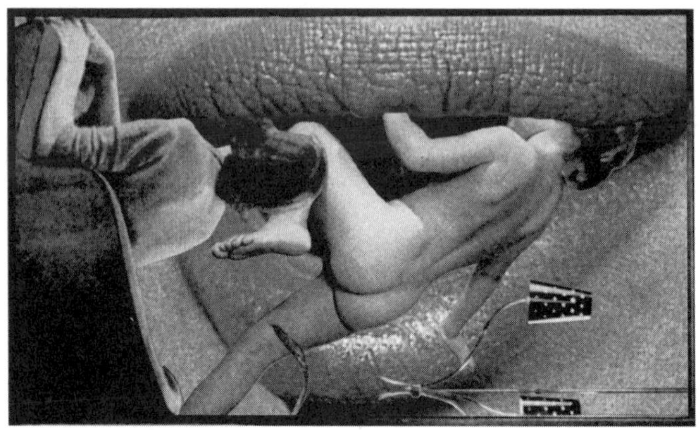

199. AS A SOAP OPERA

Rex Rory, flamboyant resident, slaps her. Punches her on the shoulders.

Nona Nova, hospital nurse, laughs at his foolish lopsided smacks.

"You no good bitch!" he yells. "You trollop! You whelp! You malfeasor! You think I'm just another one of your toys you can play with and throw away? You think you can sleep with me and turn round and sleep with my sister, my own *sister*, Rita Rory, without a thought? Well, you can't! You're gonna pay for this! You're gonna wished you never laid eyes on me!"

Nona Nova flashes him one of her flawless patented grins. "And how, pray tell, do you think you're going to accomplish *that*?" she asks.

"Like *this!*" Rex Rory, flamboyant resident, shouts, flipping an oily blue revolver into view.

113. REVOLVER

"And so," Paul McCartney says, interviewing (if Ker's not mistaken) Marshall McLuhan on some minimalist powder-blue set, "the thing is, aren't we talking about an ideological shift in the social dominant, really?"

"Er, um, right," McLuhan says, running a nervous hand across his salt-and-pepper hair, obviously surprised to find himself talking to this rock legend. "Because, um, well, all media, from the phonetic alphabet to the computer, are extensions of man that cause deep and lasting changes in him and transform his environment. Such an extension is an intensification, an amplification of an organ, sense or function, and whenever it takes place, the central nervous system appears to institute a self-protective *numbing* of the affected area . . ."

"Insulates and anesthetizes it from conscious awareness, doesn't it?"

"A process rather like that which occurs to the body under shock or stress conditions, or to the mind in line with the Freudian concept of repression."

"So what you're saying, really, is that multiple subjectivities can't articulate their circumscribed 'reality'—to employ a perhaps-outdated social construct—can they, until they've moved beyond that positional matrix?"

McLuhan shoots McCartney a half-lidded suspicious glance.

"The . . . um . . . right . . . Most people cling to what I call the rearview-mirror view of their world. By this I mean to say that because of the invisibility of any environment during the period of its innovation, man is only consciously aware of the environment that has *preceded* it. In other words, an environment becomes fully visible only when it has been superseded by a new environment. Thus we're always one step behind in our view of the world."

"So what you're suggesting is that the ideological imperative becomes recontextualized only through a spacio-temporal re-configuration?"

"I . . . hey, who are you?"

McLuhan stops with the hand thing.

"Paul."

"No. I'm serious. Who are you . . . *really*?"

"I'm, em, Paul. Paul McCartney. The Beatle and all?"

"You're not."

"I am."

"You're not. Paul doesn't talk like that. He doesn't . . . He's not as . . ."

"There's more to Paul than meets the eye, man."

"Stop it. You're scaring me."

"Have you ever wondered why he never shows any signs of aging, for example?"

"Stop it."

"Oh, sure, a little gray hair like five years ago, and then . . . poof . . . nothing. Remember? And that baby face . . ."

"Stop it!"

"Exactly the same as a decade ago, isn't it . . . and as the decade before that. I mean, compare his holding-power to that of Keith Richards, you know, and what do you see?"

"I'm covering my ears here and whistling to myself."

"Freaky, isn't it?"

"Hmmmmm hmmmmmm . . ."

"I've got two words for you."

"I see your mouth moving but I refuse to listen."

"Tick tick."

"Hmmmmmmmm hmmmmmmmm hmmmmmmmm . . ."

"Tick tick. Tick Tick."

"Hmmmmmmmm hmmmmmmmm hmmmmmmmm . . ."

268. NATURE IS NOT NICE

How many teenagers are left?

First four. Then three. Then two.

Now only one.

The most beautiful. Fair angel. Eighteen and mostly naked. Lace panties and bra. Bespattered with mud. Wet blond hair matted to face. Trickles of water and tears zigging down her cheeks. Trapped in the barn of the desolate farm. Stalked by Zodiac Killer, homicidal maniac.

Violent rainstorm crashing outside.

Lightning.

In each enormous flash a huge shadow looms closer.

She screams piercingly. She crawls. She stands. She sits, paralyzed by mortality.

Zodiac Killer wields a pitchfork in one hand and a whirring chainsaw in the other.

He towers over her.

He's laughing.

The teenager must learn how to lose gracefully.

Because in her back pocket she's carrying a nearly used-up tube of gash-red lipstick and, if she's not murdered right this minute, Zodiac Killer knows, she will drive to the coast two months hence to quietly reflect upon her past and contemplate her future options (a major in business at Slippery Rock Community College? a major in communications at Fairleigh Dickinson?) and that tube will accidentally work its way out of her back pocket and pop onto the sand where the cute little French boy who starred in that commercial for Zerp will, while vacationing on Coney Island with his parents during his first holiday to the U.S. (in celebration of his ascending career), pick it up forty-one days later and chuck it as far as he can into the Atlantic Ocean on a reflexive whim.

Little will he comprehend as he does so, though, that that tube will comprise the last piece of human shit thrown into the ocean before all the human shit thrown into the ocean over all the millennia of human shit-in-the-ocean-throwing finally reaches some critical mass, generating a molecular flashpoint where all the nascent waste-nanites flushed down secret-lab toilets over the last decade off the coast of New Jersey will merge with various contraceptives, industrial sludge, artificial fruit juices for kids, and cheap metals (including that tube of gash-red lipstick) and become in one shocking burst sentient, nor that that mess's first thought will concern destroying the ignorant lower life forms hogging all the good dry space on the planet, meaning mostly humanoids, and hence launching a massive assault on the human race, which it will do by first sneaking up on and attacking unsuspecting swimmers, then unsuspecting surfers, then small-boaters, then large-shippers, and, on one momentous day in August, by loosing a blitzkrieg no one could foresee on Tokyo, New York, and London, resulting within fewer than four months in the earth having been turned into a big ball of very intelligent gray nano-goo.

3. PRIME: TIME: LIVE

Bad would have to be an understatement for how Ker feels.

Something evil has begun transpiring in his bowels. Plus his head feels like someone has inserted a hose through his left ear and pumped his cranial cavity full of pink insulation.

Plus, if he's not mistaken, he can't feel his feet anymore.

He thinks one word to himself: *bathroom.*

As he shakily rises to propel himself posthaste down the hall, the pounding at the front door commences.

172. AS SEEN ON TV

Tribal drums and primitive wails blossom.

Colors whirl.

Black men in grass skirts and jangling brass earrings, bracelets, and necklaces dance wildly around a bonfire, shaking spears, lifting knees, hooting and jabbering at the nightspirits.

Their earlobes hang to their jawbones.

Scars mark their cheeks.

Only the whites of their eyes show.

They leap and caper around this naked pale body tied to the ground, ready for the sacrifice, his arms stretched out to his sides, his legs wide apart, his anxious face alert . . . familiar . . . very familiar . . .

"Way-hate a sec here," Ker says aloud, halfway out of his bean-bag chair.

He leans forward, aware of sick sweat forming across his upper lip, squints, focuses, and sees . . . a-and sees . . . *himself* there, his own eyes looking back at him, terrified . . .

"Oh, *fuck!!!!!*"

13. HE DO THE POLICE IN DIFFERENT VOICES

Thomas Stearns Eliot, born in St. Louis on September 26, 1888, was one of the greatest

222. KNOW YOUR INNER CHILD

166. THE GREAT WHEEL SPINS

A car burns out of control. Upside down. A bus on top of it. An orange and black and umber and saffron fireball.

But whose car?

Where?

Under what circumstances?

Who's inside?

58. LOVEBOAT

It's too late.

The barrel-chested man in the black cowboy hat fires.

China crashes.

Crystal splinters.

A chair cracks against the floor.

Buh-but the mother in the white cowboy hat fires first.

With her tommy gun.

"*Uggghhhh!*" the barrel-chested man in the white cowboy hat cries, astounded, chest riddled with bullets. He slumps to his knees. "Mama . . ." he says, surprised.

Pitches forward.

Expires.

Mother laughs, embraces the barrel-chested man in the black cowboy hat, united with her lover at last.

99. NATURE IS NOT NICE

Ker starts off down the hall, something expanding in his bowels like a film of a blossoming black carnation, only the pounding at the front door gets louder and more insistent.

He groans, stops, turns, sort of shuffle-hops a couple of paces toward the living room, thinks better of it, turns, trots toward the bathroom, halts when the pounding erupts onto banging, begins worrying about Syndi again (it simply has to be time for her to get home . . . he needs to remember to glance at the clock in the bedroom as he passes), halts, cradles his belly like a pregnant woman, turns, shuffle-hops towards the front door, earnestly contemplates embarrassing himself in front of a stranger, concludes this couldn't be Syndi, she just wouldn't pound like that, turns, trots toward the bathroom, halts when he realizes she wouldn't pound like that *unless it was an emergency*, turns, shuffle-hops toward the front door, undoes the two bolts and chain and lock, cracks it open, and . . . *BLAM!!!*

In explodes Zodiac Killer, and, fuck, is he big . . . seven feet tall if an inch, and somehow that ski mask makes him look that much bigger, and the huge Bowie knife, too, which he's currently resting against Ker's throat, having with his forearm pinned Ker to the wall, and he's smiling . . .

"What have you done with Syndi?" Ker gurgles.

"That her name, huh? Cute thing . . ."

It strikes Ker he's never thought about Zodiac Killer's breath before, but now understands it has the same moisture and fecal reek as the air maybe two inches above a garbage dump on the outskirts of São Paulo on a hot summer's afternoon.

Ker gurgles some more in anger.

He shuts his eyes.

His bowels round the homestretch toward a pure plasma state.

Zodiac Killer chortles.

"She . . . liked it," he whispers tenderly in Ker's left ear, "is the thing. Asked for more. Died with a grin on her face. Know what she said before I hoisted her off the floor with the noose? Before she shat herself and died, grinning? 'Do me harder, sweetmeat. Do me . . .' Hic-hic-hic. Hic-hic-hic."

Ker opens his eyes.

A fairly large rivulet of blood is running out of Zodiac Killer's right nostril, is the first thing he sees.

Next he catches sight of that mean fire poker jutting out of the homicidal maniac's head like some weird tv antenna.

Next he understands, very briefly, that, despite Zodiac Killer's breath, the guy really takes very good care of his teeth.

Because those teeth are all on display right now, as Zodiac Killer begins to squeak like a stepped-on mouse and spin around simultaneously, at which point Ker sort of slides down the wall like a slice of peanut-buttered bread, and he notices . . . hey, way-hate a sec here . . . Ker's suddenly wearing *lace panties and bra* . . . how the hell did *that* happen? . . . and his own pert teenage breasts fascinate him so much he can't help lifting a palm to cup one and cop a quick feel, only . . . *whump* . . . the chair shatters across Zodiac Killer's back . . . and there, above and left . . . who *is* that? . . . oh yeah, none other than the strikingly handsome nineteen-year-old baby-faced boy, Keane or Keir or Kendall or Kilian or Kipp or Kyle, whom Zodiac Killer shishkebabed earlier in the made-for-tv movie with another (and, in this case, barbed) redhot fire poker . . . and yet . . . and yet . . . he's *walking* . . . Keane or Keir or Kendall or Kilian or Kipp or Kyle's inching along, poker still sticking through his chest, not quite dead yet, still time for one last act of really impressive selfless heroism . . .

Flawless teeth in his grin, too, the drop-dead gorgeous guy raises two fingers to his forehead in a flip salute to posterity, gingerly releases an oily blue revolver from his back pocket, and takes aim.

"Yippie-kay-eh, motherfucker," he says.

And pulls the trigger.

But misses.

532. AS SEEN ON TV

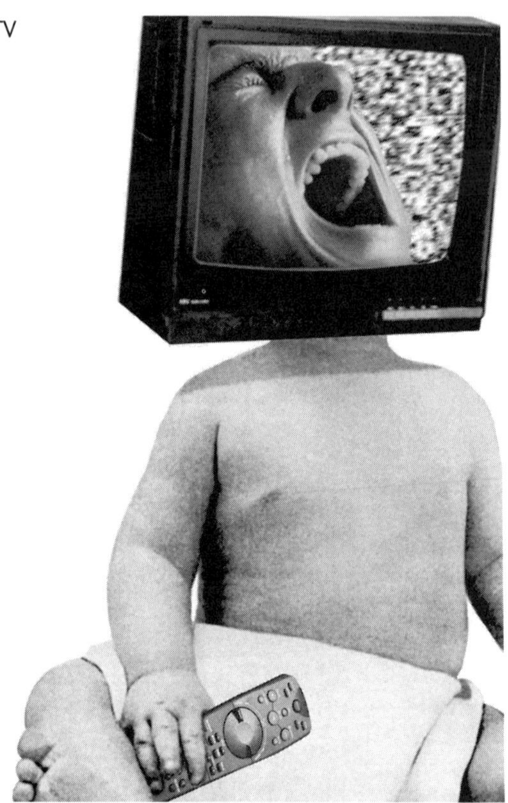

4. HE DO THE POLICE IN DIFFERENT VOICES

Rex Rory, flamboyant resident, releases an oily blue revolver from his back pocket, takes aim, and shoots Nona Nova, hospital nurse, once, just below her pert twentysomething left breast.

Not before Nona Nova, though, releases an oily blue revolver from her . . . where, exactly? . . . the logistics for this are somehow eluding Ker . . . and shoots him point blank in the groin.

Twice.

They fall to their respective knees.

"You rascally knave!" he shouts.

"You miserable miscreant!" she shouts.

"Strumpet!" he shouts, blood bubbling to his lips.

"Beetle-headed whoreson!" she shouts, unable to catch her breath.

"Worsted-stocking beggar!" he shouts, falling over on his side.

"Reprobate cuckold!" she shouts, toppling over on her face.

"Mama?" the barrel-chested man in the black cowboy hat asks tentatively, poking his head into the women's restroom at the hospital. "Daddy? That you?"

249. THE DISCOVERY: CHANNEL

The monstrous great blue whale hangs under the ocean, ultramarine, pine green, indigo, gray, singing for its mate.

207. ADDRESS AT VISION 31

The great wheel spins. The audience shouts insanely. The game show host smiles confidently. Madge Moertel, fifty-seven, from Whitewater, Wisconsin, with a son in Attica, jumps up and down, her fat chugging, and claps her tiny hands in glee. The wheel spits fire. The wheel spits flame. Lights flash like lightning, and . . . slowly . . .

The wheel clicks to a halt, its arrow pointing to JACKPOT.

Sirens shriek. Buzzers trill. Alarms rattle.

Madge Moertel leaps into the air like an African chieftain. Bounds into the arms of the host. Her daughter rockets out of the audience and slaps onto the bi-hominidal cluster like a magnet.

Madge Moertel wins a dream vacation to Haiti.

Madge Moertel wins a year's supply of cat food for her dog.

Madge Moertel's face sprouts a flower. Her fingers sprout diamonds. Her eyes roll up under her lids.

She ignites.

A tremendous explosion follows: orange and black and umber and saffron fireball.

All around her people duck and cover.

33. WHITE QUEEN: BODILESSNESS: DARK

Which is when the ants come.

Ker lying flat on his back in his lace bra and panties beside his bean-bag chair in the living room, unable to move so much as an eyelid, watching the ceiling swarm with black ants. It seems like the ceiling doesn't even really exist anymore, that it's been insectivally devoured, that the ants have somehow *become* the ceiling through the act of ingesting it, a vibrant black undulating mass . . . which would have been awfully unpleasant in itself, no doubt, except that wasn't all.

The ants? They aren't just *above* his head. They're *inside* his head, too.

Ker can feel them skittering over the bones that comprise his skull where all that facial and cranial skin of his used to hang. He can feel them seething in place of the tongue in his mouth. They rush through his sinuses and over the backs of his eyeballs. They migrate up his otic canals, nibble through his ear drums, make burger of his hammers and anvils and stirrups and cochleae, single-file down his Eustachian tubes, and blast up his auditory nerves in a screech of B-film noise.

They assemble massive ant ranches in the creases of his cerebral cortex and the queen, obese and gloopy and gnarled like a big white turd, excavates his cerebellum and wraps her starched napkin around her horrible neck that joins her horrible cyborgish head to her horrible cyborgish thorax and picks up her mandibular knife and fork and goes to gustative town while birthing thousands of larval rice-eggs every minute, which is awful, godawful, but not as awfully godawful as when her troops force their way down Ker's esophagus in one big ramrod and then branch out into his lungs, ripping their way through mealy tissue and planting hundreds of larvae in some of the smaller less important semi-mucusy lung sacs, meaning Ker begins to cough, feeling like he can't catch his breath, till he forgets about that slight discomfort because they've also made their way into his heart, it feels like, though maybe it's just the lower reaches of his trachea, at which point he lurches into a full-blown grand mal seizure, or what from his perspective feels like a full-blown grand mal seizure, but can't be, in point of fact, since he still retains a semblance of consciousness.

Except what *really* scares him is when they get into his stomach, which about now feels like he's just gargled with a bottle of Sani-Flush laced with pins and thumbtacks, this flaming mass of damnation hissing into volcanic steam clouds when it hits meaty bottom and pretty much vaporizes his gall bladder and liver, and you don't even want to ask about his bile duct or poor little fried knot of duodenum, before whooming full-speed-ahead into his intestines, both large and small, like so much superheated plasma, causing him instantaneously to go liquid, simultaneously projectile vomiting blood-ants from his mouth, on the one hand, and spewing them in a hot muddy red jet from his anus, on the other, before what *really* spooks him happens, which is that he next just sort of goes—what's the word?—supernova.

One second he's there and the next he detonates, ka-*blam!*, covering the ceiling, which has become ants, and the walls, which have become ants, and the floors, which have become ants, with, weh-hell, ants and more ants and chunks of organs and flaps of skin and wads of hair, *his* organs and skin and hair, which now sprout compound eyes and six legs apiece and antennae and almost imperceptibly small stingers on their bottoms a-and start tooling away, single-file, a miniature battalion of buggish body parts marching in different directions, merging with the ant-soup all around them, the ant sea, the great ocean of Antlantis, a-and Ker lies there in his lace bra and panties, terrified, flat on his back, just watching his shredded selves disappear into the deep, into the dark, into that huge black nidus of bloodcurdling selflessness . . .

85. THE DISCOVERY: CHANNEL

"Ker?" Syndi asks tentatively, poking her head through the apartment door. "Ker? That you? Hey, happy birthday, lover! . . . Hey . . . but . . . uh, what's all this?"

128. SWEEPS: NEWS: TIME

We exchange memes in the night, with our bodies' erotic contact, just as bacteria exchange genes . . .

37. TIME FAMINE

200. THE LOVEBOAT

How many teenagers are left?
First four. Then three. Then two.
Now only one.
The most beautiful. Fair angel. Eighteen and mostly naked.

Lace panties and over-large Sick Poppies t-shirt of this black woodcut of this male bedbug stabbing its beak into this female bedbug's abdomen, preparing to release its sperm into her wound and bloodstream.

Wire-rimmed glasses bespattered with mud. Wet ponytail come undone. Honey hair matted to face.

It's . . . hey . . . it's *Syndi!*

Ker'd recognize her anywhere.

She's trapped in the barn of the desolate farm, stalked by Zodiac Killer, homicidal maniac.

Violent rainstorm crashing outside.

Lightning.

In each enormous flash a huge shadow looms closer.

She screams piercingly. She crawls. She stands. She sits, paralyzed by mortality, preparing to learn how to lose gracefully.

Zodiac Killer wields a pitchfork in one hand (Timex on wrist, you can't miss it) and a whirring chainsaw in the other.

He towers over her, laughing.

And then, unexpectedly, he chucks the pitchfork to his left, the chainsaw to his right.

Syndi cringes.

The chainsaw sputters and dies.

Zodiac Killer reaches up, grabs hold of his ski-mask, and tugs.

Beneath the mask is . . . is . . . weh-hell . . . it's *Ker!*

Syndi looks up, disbelieving at first, then a grin gradually spreads across her sweet countenance.

She breaks into laughter.

Stands, enters his parted arms.

"Ker," she says, "Ker . . ."

"It's okay, babe," Ker says, wearing his beige sweater with maroon stripes, "we made it."

They embrace.

They kiss.

On the lips.

Syndi reaches for his belt.

Ker reaches for her pert teenage breasts. For her firm belly. For the astonishing curve of her spine.

33. STEAL MY THOUGHTS FOR MONEY

97. LOVEBOAT: THE SEQUEL

Kerwin Penumbro feels like a million bucks.

OOO. IMMORTALITY: STEALTH

The phone rings.

Ker's eyes pop open.

He's been sleeping.

The room's dark except for the blue photonic haze from the Stealth's screen.

What time is it?

He reaches over and picks up the receiver.

"Myellow?"

"Mr. Penumbro?"

"Um, yeah?" he says, blinking himself awake.

"Mr. Penumbro, this is the police calling. You've been listed as next of kin on Syndi Shogunn's living will."

"What?"

"Ms. Shogunn was attacked in the parking lot of the police station, Mr. Penumbro. The Zodiac Killer. She's in a coma at the hospital. You should get down here fast as you can . . ."

59. MIND AS CATHODE-RAY TUBE

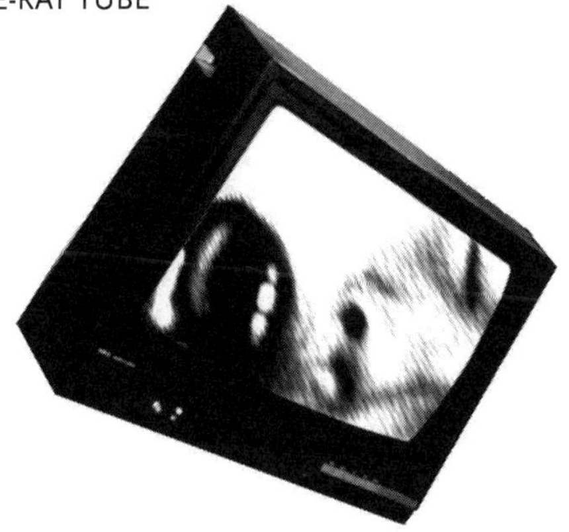

164. DELTA: ART ALLUSION: SWEEPS

"Claude," Claude's father Clyde, man with the knowing smile, says to the cute little French boy from the soft-drink commercial as he steps off the wedge-shaped spaceship, all happy endings, "you know I love you."

"I love you too, dad," Claude says, wearing a beige sweater with maroon stripes.

They grin.

They embrace.

They kiss.

On the lips.

Claude reaches for Clyde's belt.

Clyde reaches for Claude's breasts. For his belly. For the astonishing curve of his spine.

13. UNCLE BUDDY'S PHANTOM FUNHOUSE

Man thus becomes the sex organs of the machine world just as the bee is of the plant world, permitting it to reproduce and constantly evolve to higher forms . . .

141. AS SEEN ON TV

The phone rings. Ker's eyes pop open. He's been sleeping. The room's dark except for the blue photonic haze from the Stealth's screen. What time is it? He reaches over and picks up the receiver. "Myellow?" "Ker?" "Um, yeah?" he says, blinking himself awake. "Ker, it's me." "Syndi?" "I'm running a little late. Be home in ten. Happy birthday, lover . . ."

177. SHE DO THE POLICE IN DIFFERENT VOICES

"I see a young woman," says psychic healer Abbey Rode, whose hair reminds Ker of a red rubber wig. Abbey has that slack-muscled serious-yet-utterly-accepting face that only drugged children and talk-show psychic healers have. Her eyes are closed in concentration. "Blond hair. Wire-rimmed glasses. She's on a farm, an isolated farm, a-and she will die tonight . . ."

209. PLAY: SIN

Zodiac Killer wields a pitchfork in one hand and a whirring chainsaw in the other.

He towers over her, laughing.

Syndi cringes.

The chainsaw flies down.

But misses.

Syndi leaps up, head-butting him in the groin, and he folds in pain. She yanks the pitchfork from his grip and drives it home, smack into the middle of his forehead.

Blood burbles from his lips.

He does that death-shudder thing people in low-budget made-for-tv movies do.

Syndi yanks out the pitchfork, reaches down, grabs hold of his ski-mask, and tugs.

Beneath the mask is . . . is . . . weh-hell . . . it's *Ker*!

Syndi stares, disbelieving at first, then a grin gradually spreads across her sweet countenance.

She breaks into laughter.

"About fucking time," she says.

999. HOPE FLOATS

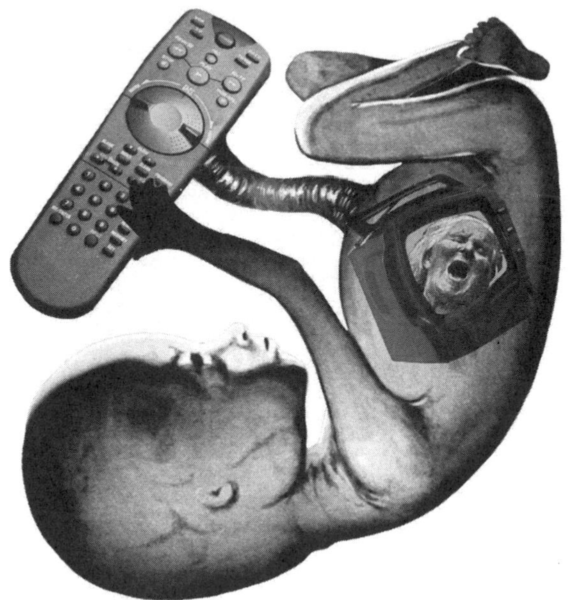

91. RUBBER WIG: ART: CRIMES

A woman with stelliform shoe-polish black hair's head derricks up and down in a man's naked lap.

The camera pans back.

A tv delivery man in khaki shirt is taking her from behind. Between his legs lies a second woman clearly wearing a cheap blond wig, lapping at the delivery man's genitals. Ker can't get a good look at her.

Buh-but, even in that wig, from this angle it looks just like . . .

217. ADDRESS AT VISION 31

The rock'n'roll star hangs under the ocean, ultramarine, pine green, indigo, gray, singing for his mate. Bubbles sizzle out of his mouth. He raises two fingers to his forehead in a flip salute to posterity, unaware of the great white shark speeding in from behind him, flawless teeth in its grin.

14. SWEEPS: AS A SOAP OPERA: VANISHING POINT

Rex Rory, behind the wheel of one of the cars (though which is unclear), perspiration sparkling on his face, fury in his eyes, hatred at mouth corners, sticks his oily blue revolver out the window and squeezes off two shots.

The glowing green delta over the city wobbles.

Cut to the two children at the control panels, faces raided with terror, clutching each other and screaming.

The ship ignites.

A tremendous explosion follows: orange and black and umber and saffron fireball.

All across the city people duck and cover, thinking they are saved from the terrible invaders, but are wrong, because a single germ from planet Zerp will survive this nuclear blaze and drift down to earth where it will land on a fifty-dollar bill extended in the hand of one Mary Christmas to pay Dick Smoker for the crack cocaine she desperately needs to feed her recent addiction following her dad's recent bizarre demise (fetish encasement; lack of breathing tubes).

The germ will be passed via that bill across the country and then across the Atlantic to Berlin in the hands of a tourist named Gaye Powwers, where it will be exchanged for deutsche marks, during which process the germ will fall on the floor, where it will wait for six more months, till a little snot-nosed girl whose name isn't important will deliberately drop a wad of Bazooka bubble-gum on it, which a Pekingese named Fopson will later that day eat, passing the germ through his system unscathed while on a train bound for Prague, in which city he will deposit said germ by means of a well-formed pile of feces on his master's nice white rug at three a.m. for no particular reason, where his master's son, Fritz, distant ancestor of Franz Kafka's bastard child, at that stage where he has to taste everything, will pick it up and actually take a bite first thing next morning, bringing the germ to consciousness as it hits those special stomach acids that spell H-U-M-A-N, at which point said germ will begin to multiply, releasing a plague that will cause people to see what happened to them four seconds ago, instead of what's happening to them right now, which will within the course of six years kill off the entire population of the planet by means of various ghastly accidents (car crashes, elevator mishaps, defenestration), paving the way for the next species to dominate the earth . . . not the cockroach, as it turns out, as many people believed, but the feathery-antennaed moth which, to this moment, had just been minding its own business, evolutionarily speaking.

777. BURNING MAN: THE SERIES

70. NATURE IS NOT NICE

Wile E. Coyote rises with great dignity, wipes the drop of whitish foam from his bottom with a handkerchief he gingerly produces . . .

from where, exactly? . . . and hobbles toward the sunset as the Roadrunner, lounging by a boulder, smirk on his beak, rests his left heel on his right knee, lights a cigarette, and begins to dream of Paul McCartney in lace bra and panties.

1. THE DISCOVERY: CHANNEL

You wait one one-thousand, two one-thousand, three, trying to believe this can't be happening.

He plummets like a starfish.

There is no white bouquet of chute, no slowing of momentum, no sound save the whipping of wind far above the tiny red, white, and blue dot.

You watch him flap his arms and kick his legs.

You watch him speeding down, faster and faster . . . shooting down . . . humming down . . . hurtling straight for the jagged rocks and shallow river threading below.

The strong current.

The icy water.

The twisted bodies of those who tried and failed before him.

Seventy feet to go . . . forty . . . twenty . . . ten . . . six . . . a-and then: *whoosh*!

A-and then: *ahhhhh*!

A-and then and then and then: he pulls the backup cord and a beautiful orange and black and umber and saffron hang-glider unfolds from his parachute pouch like wings.

He skims the whitewater, zips over the jagged rocks, ascends above the pine trees in a miraculous arc, higher and higher, fair angel.

As he swoops up toward you, you see his face . . . his familiar face . . . his very familiar face. Beneath the lightning bolts on his helmet you make out Ker's features, those flawless teeth in his grin.

He zooms closer, raises two fingers to his forehead in a flip salute to posterity, and when you blink again he's . . .

Gone.

33. HOPE FLOATS

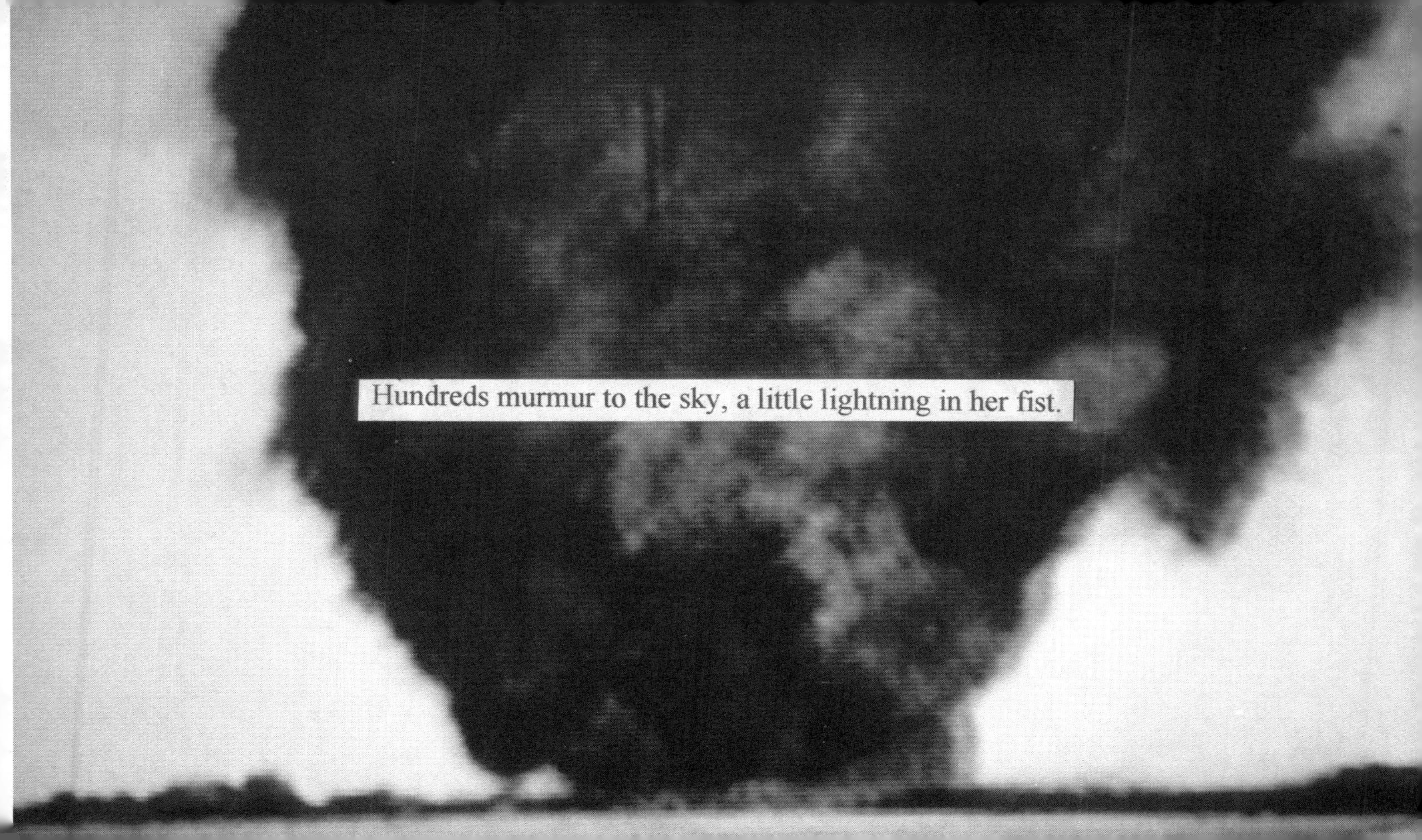

Hundreds murmur to the sky, a little lightning in her fist.

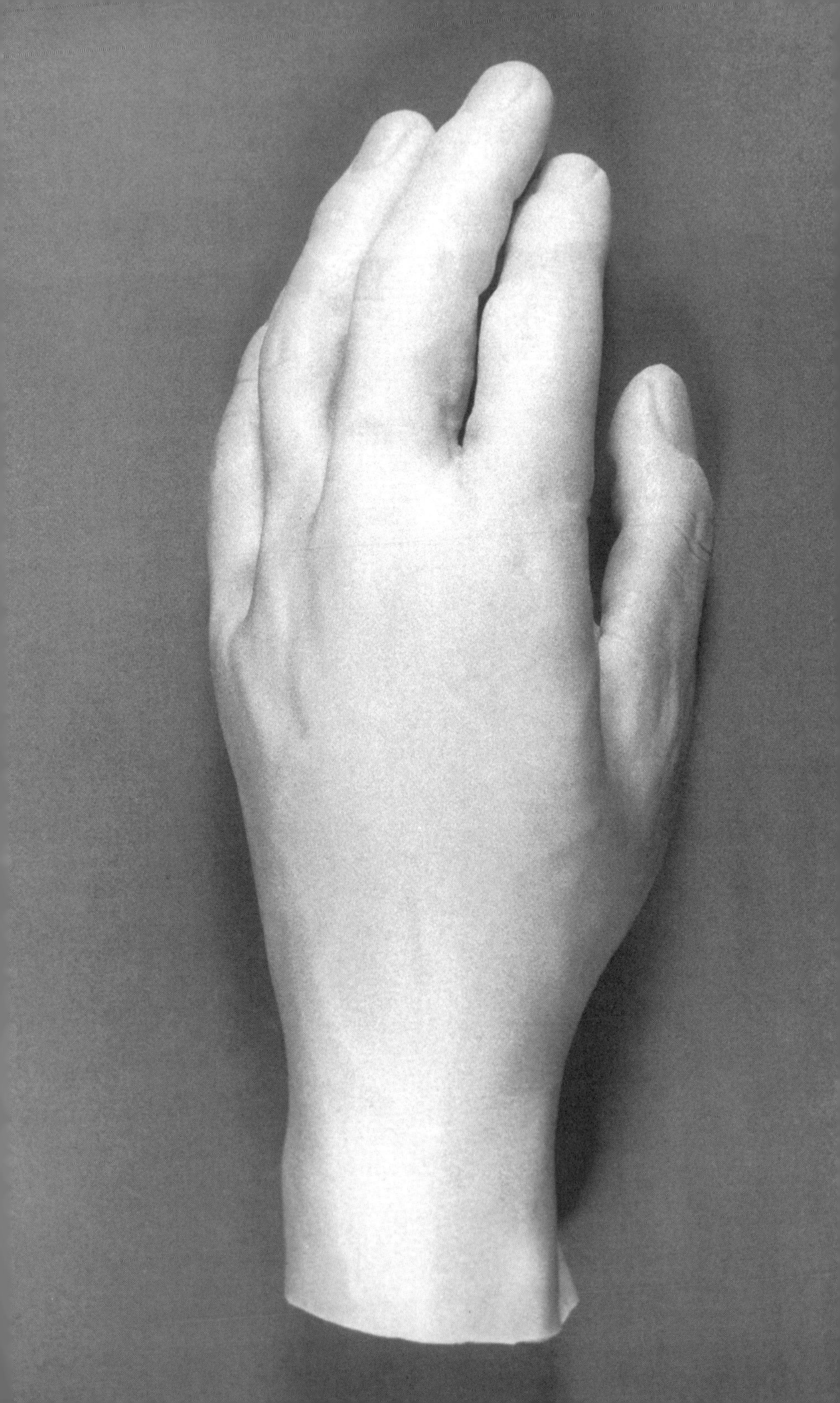

The breath of sleeping children almost too loud.

what it lacks

MEAGAN ATIYEH

1 How am I to begin it? she asks.
There is a small room sided with windows in
morning. A man and woman at a desk piled with books
(Macbeth). Beyond the room may be a vast structure abraded
by time, halls so long they seem to run empty. A place of
such exotic promise that all the children come to search it.
2 The day dawned black and chill, he says, and
pauses for her to take his words down.
3 Gradually, she continues, the dark bar on the
horizon became clear. Anything may be out the window.
4 He stops her: The earth immediately about the
door was bare. It had a patina, as though from the soles of
bare feet in generations.
5 Is it worthwhile? she asks, What is the point of it
6 all? She rings for a maid. Life escapes, she thinks, Woman
thinks. He does. Organ plays. She writes. They say: She
sings. Night speaks. They miss . . . . Each other in opposing
gestures within the room. Do you know this well?
7 But he will not stop for her. The day dawned black
and chill, he writes. Each in its ordered place. A moving
wall of gray light out of the Northeast which, instead of
dissolving into moisture, seemed to disintegrate into minute
and venomous particles.
A child playing tamely in the hall has his ear to the
8 heavy door. Inexorable veracity, the child whispers.
9 Enigmatic profundity, the man retorts. There are
so many children listening at the door. They are
choreographed, just as the two within the room are to one

another—moving slowly in this strange topography. But without care.

10 Raising a glass of water for a pill the maid has brought, she is aware of her own restlessness, a vague and cloudy nature full of sediment, full of doubt, full of phrases and notes to be made in pocketbooks. The folds of the curtain become still, she thinks, statuesque. The paperweight on the table hardens; the threads on the curtain sparkle; everything becomes definite, external, a scene in which I have no part. She moves to the window: I rose, therefore I left him.

There is her detachment.

11 Where he pays her absence no mind. He writes: A big man who appeared to have been shaped of some substance whose particles would not or did not cohere to one another or to the frame which supported it. His skin was dead looking and hairless; dropsicle too, he moved with a shambling gait like a trained bear. His hair was pale and fine. His eyes were clear, of the pale sweet blue of cornflowers, his thick mouth hung open, drooling a little.

12 A scene in which I had no part, the woman thinks.

13 He writes: Ben sat beside the stove. He sat loosely, utterly motionless save for his head, which made a continual bobbing sort of movement as he watched Dilsey with his sweet vague gaze.

14 She turns to watch him as he writes. One pellet was a man, she thinks, one was a woman. We are all pellets. We are all phrases in his story, things he writes down under A or B. He tells our story with extraordinary understanding, except of what we most feel. For he does not need us. He is never at our mercy.

15 . . . It was as if even eagerness were musclebound in him too, and hunger itself inarticulate, not knowing it as hunger.

16 They miss. She tells him.

Their room is still. The children, as they are bound to, have been frightened by the plainness in her voice as a mother's sad singing in the afternoon.

17 . . . Luster fed him with skill and detachment. Now and then his attention would return long enough to enable him to feint the spoon and cause Ben to close his mouth on upon the empty air.

18 And I eat, she thinks, I gradually lose all knowledge of particulars as I eat. I am becoming weighed down with food. These delicious mouthfuls of roast duck, fitly piled with vegetables, following each other in exquisite rotation of warmth, weight, sweet and bitter, past my palate, down my gullet, into my stomach, have stabilized my body. I feel quiet, gravity, control. All is solid now. But what particular name are we to call it?

A child whispers to her alone, so clearly the small
19 warm breath can reach her ear: The algebraic sign of an intention . . . a lie made manifest.

20 But I begin to doubt the fixity of tables, she tells the child, the reality of here and now, to tap my knuckles smartly upon the edges of apparently solid objects and say, 'Are you hard?' I have seen so many different things, have made so many different sentences. I am lost in the process of eating and drinking and rubbing my eyes.

But the child has left. A sense of something that cannot be found, told, touched, or remembered in whole.

21 His story of the monster builds: Ben sat in the chair, his big soft hands dangling between his knees, moaning faintly. Suddenly he wept, a slow, bellowing sound, meaningless and sustained.

22 Now is life very solid or shifting? she asks, I am haunted by the two contradictions.

23 . . . Hopeless and prolonged. It was nothing. Just sound. It might have been all the time and injustice and sorrow become vocal for an instant by a conjunction of planets.

24 Yet these roaring waters upon which we build our crazy platforms are more stable than the wild, the weak and inconsequential cries that we utter when, trying to speak,

we rise; when we reason and jerk out these false sayings, I
am this, I am that!' Speech is false, she says to her partner.
25 . . . That slow hoarse sound that ships make, that
seems to begin before the sound itself has started, seems to
cease before the sound itself has stopped. The grave hopeless
sound of all voiceless misery under the sun.

26 I will reduce you to order, she says, laughing. To
translate that poem: A plate was like a white lake.

27 . . . For an instant Ben sat in utter hiatus. Then he
bellowed. The man pauses his words to light a cigarette and
follow his partner's practiced movements about the room .
28 . .bellow on bellow, his voice mounted, with scarce interval
for breath. There was more than astonishment in it, it was
horror; shock; agony, eyeless, tongueless, just sound.

She moves downstage towards their audience, the
29 lights pushing at her body. There is a red carnation in that
vase she says to us. A single flower as we sat here waiting,
but now a seven-sided flower, many petalled, red, puce,
purple-shaded, stiff with silver tinted leaves—a whole flower
to which every eye brings its own contribution.

seeking ursa minor

COLIN DICKEY

I tell her, I love you and we're happy.

It's morning and I say, What should we do now? and Tina says, I want to be fucked. Then treated like a princess. You can buy me breakfast.

At breakfast I stare off into space.

I love you and we're happy.

Tina asks, Are you okay? Her metallic smell lingers on my hands and she still has Fuck Hair. The sun comes in the window between us in the diner and it's hard to look straight at Tina without squinting. My back is raked with rivulets left by her nails so I can't lean back on anything. She asks if I'm okay in the same way that she asked if I was okay an hour ago after she bit my tongue slightly. Occasionally I taste the blood in my mouth. In an instant: the look of her hair, her smell on my fingers, the feel of my back, the sound of her voice, the taste of my blood. All five senses reminding me of the sex I can't get out of my mind like the words that I can't get out of my head either, these words which are not the problem like the sex is not the problem, but which nevertheless remind me that there's something growing between us which could be love but isn't.

Let my right hand wither. Let my tongue cleave to the roof of my mouth.

I love you and we're happy.

The food comes. The waitress brings me my Dr. Pepper and more coffee for Tina and this isn't working anymore. The way love works in America at the end of the twentieth century, we're told to either be excited or comfortable, either desire or security, but there's nothing between this and when neither of these quite fit then it just doesn't work, and this isn't working anymore. The waitress asks, Do you need anything else? and I think maybe the only thing that would make me happy with Tina is to do something so violent to her that we could be sure there was no love or anything else between us. The waitress turns to the television on the wall. There's the weather forecast and the waitress says, It's going to be clear tonight for once; it's not going to rain.

After sex Tina cries and I ask, Why, and she says, I don't know. If she's crying because she's happy or because she's sad, either way, it's not good news.

We eat quietly over the silence of our not quite working relationship. When I tell her I love her, she smiles then I stare off into space. Behind her head on the wall are three holes made by pushpins forming a small neat line.

Remember, O Lord, against the Edomites, the day of Jerusalem, how they said, Rase it, rase it! Down to the foundations!

Do you remember—I ask Tina—it was like our second or third date, and I told you how I always feel like I'm just waiting for my turn to talk, that it was rare that I actually cared what the other person is saying?

Okay, she says. Yes, she says. Yes, I remember that conversation.

The way that people walk up to you and say, Guess what? And you say, What, then they unload on you all this fabulous information about their life that you really didn't want to know. No one wants a conversation anymore.

Yes, Tina says, and you said you didn't want to do that with me.

Because, I say, you said—although you said this later—you said that a relationship is built on communication. You said it was a cliché that was true. You said you wanted a relationship that was direct and immediate, where we were one, and you could tell me everything, and the only way to do that was to keep the lines of communication open, to always be talking and opening up to each other.

And she says, Yes, I remember that. Why, what did you want to talk about?

And I say, Nothing.

What happens when you run out of the words to describe what's in your head? Or the words are just wrong, and the words end up driving you farther apart instead of closer together? I don't ask Tina this because these words are also wrong and she won't understand what I mean which will make things worse.

She says, Nothing? Are you sure?

O daughter of Babylon, you devastator! Happy shall he be who requites you with what you have done to us!

And I say, Yes. All I wanted to say was that I love you. And that I'm happy with you.

Happy shall he be who takes your little ones and dashes them against the rocks!

As I'm saying all of this, I'm looking at the drops of condensation that my Dr. Pepper has left on the table. I dot little pinpricks of water that shine in the sunlight, until they start to look like a constellation. I say to Tina, Look the Big Dipper, and Tina says, The Big Dipper's handle curves up, not down; that's Ursa Minor. With my now wet finger I trace the constellation made out of water and connect the pinprick stars on the table between us, and Tina says, I want to go out to the hills and look at the stars tonight. She says, It's been a long time living in Portland since I've actually seen stars and the waitress said it'll be clear. I tell Tina, Okay. I look back at the three black holes on the wall behind her. Because of the sunlight it's easier to look at the wall than at Tina.

The dots on the wall look like Orion's belt, so close together and angled slightly. Orion, unlike Big and Little Dippers, is easy to recognize. Orion is everyone's patron constellation because it's the one everyone can find: look for three stars in a row and you have it. Trinities are easy.

Tina asks, If each time you're in love it's a totally different experience, how is it that the actions always end up feeling the same? Holding hands is always holding hands, a kiss on the neck is a kiss on the neck.

Bullshit, I say.

Before we were in love we were lying in bed after sex and I ask Tina about her past boyfriends. Do you miss them or do you miss having a warm body sleeping next to you? I'm looking at the body pillow she bought after her last boyfriend to take up the absence in the bed. She says, I miss something distinctly male. But that was before we were in love.

Now it's different.

Now the water from the constellation is cooling on my finger and I watch the waitress coming over. Tina says, When you have sex with me do you think of other women?

No.

Are you sure?

I'm happy with you.

I think of other men.

The waitress asks if we need anything else.

We're fine, I say. We're doing great.

More Dr. Pepper?

That'd be great.

What the hell do you mean you think of other men? I ask when the waitress is gone. Are you trying to piss me off?

Tina flinches like I've hit her. We look at each other.

Stop crying, I say. We're happy.

By the waters of Babylon, there we sat down and wept, when we remembered Zion.

On the willows there we hung up our harps.

What the hell do you mean, you think of other men? I ask again.

Not intentionally, she says. I just want to be open with you, Tina says. I just wanted you to know, she says.

For there our captors required of us songs, and our tormentors mirth, saying, Sing us one of the songs of Zion!

Past boyfriends or others?

Past lovers. It's not like I'm fantasizing about other guys. It's just that you don't fuck someone for over three years and then not ever think of them during sex.

I don't? I ask.

You're saying you never think about other women?

We're happy.

Is that a no?

Yes.

Liar, she says. Hypocrite, she says.

I love you and we're happy.

How shall we sing the Lord's song in a foreign land?

When I look at the television on the wall I see sexy girls or people in love. And products. Love and sex are good for selling products; that's probably all they're good for. Every time I forget this I seem to get myself in trouble.

I look at Tina. I have to squint in the sunlight.

If there was love between us, it's dying.

This isn't working anymore. Whatever we're doing to each other, it's no good anymore.

Nietzsche says whatever is done from love always occurs beyond good and evil.

I think he's wrong.

Good and evil are the wrong words. Love and happiness are the wrong words. Tina and I are the wrong words. I look back at the TV and I look at the holes on the wall and I look at the waitress but when I struggle to look into Tina's eyes there's something between us as big as light years and the quickly evaporating constellation on the table.

The waitress asks if she can get us anything else.

No, we're fine.

We're happy.

If I forget thee, O Jerusalem, let my right hand wither!

Let my tongue cleave to the roof of my mouth, If I do not remember you, If I do not set Jerusalem above my highest joy!

*

From Abrams Planetarium Skywatcher's Diary; Thursday, February 25th: *Tonight brilliant Venus is just over 2 degrees above Jupiter. Watch these two planets spread one degree farther apart with each passing day. The Moon is in ESE to SE, with the Gemini twins, Castor above Pollux, to the Moon's left, and Procyon below the Moon. Betelgeuse, Procyon and the brilliant twinkling Sirius, the 'Dog Star' 36 degrees to Moon's lower right, form the nearly equilateral Winter Triangle.*

Thirty minutes west of Portland there are hills amongst the wineries and that night we drive out of the city, up into these hills at the base of the Coast Range. We drive until the asphalt ends and then park in the dust next to a field, where there are no direct lights but light spills into the car from the city and the sky. Looking through the windshield you can see all of the Tualatin Valley below you, and in the distance the orange glow of Portland. There's a moment of space between us and then almost simultaneously Tina and I recline our seats slightly so we can look out through the moonroof at all of the tiny lights above our head, all of the stars we can't see from the city because of the orange canopy sky which makes the little flecks of light invisible.

Tina calls this light pollution.

I call it city glow. She finds this term immensely humorous.

Most euphemisms are, she says.

What makes it a euphemism? I ask.

She says, I prefer to cut through the crap.

Why is it crap? You look at the city and there's something new added to the environment, a new physical feature. You add light. Why is this polluting? Polluting is like mixing categories. It's not like you're menstruating in the temple.

Tina laughs again, which is a euphemism for drop the subject.

This makes me laugh, but it's a bitter cheated laugh. I look up at the moon and stars, thinking about names.

The Moon is in ESE to SE, with the Gemini twins, Castor above Pollux, to the Moon's left, and Procyon below the Moon.

I still can never remember which is the Big Dipper and which is the Little Dipper, I tell Tina.

Tina points. That's the North Star, which is the end of the Little Dipper.

She leans over and unbuttons my shirt cuff, and folds it back to reveal my wrist. She buries her teeth into my skin, in between the watchband and the palm, not quite enough to draw blood but enough to leave two crooked crescents that are black now but will be purple and red and blue tomorrow in daylight.

This is not erotic or pleasurable for me in any way.

She lets go of me and says, The two stars at the end of the cup in the Big Dipper, Dubhe and Merak, point straight to the North Star. The North Star is also Sirius, or the Dog Star, or Polaris, or Alruccabah, Cynosaura, Phoenice, the Lodestar, Tramontana, or Yilduz, or Mismar.

The way she rattles off names sounds like a lecture: a monotone dispersal of information, the way a weatherman or a waitress might talk.

I ask her, How do you know all of these names?

She continues to roll up my sleeve, folding the cuff over and over again to expose more of my arm. Midway up my bicep the sleeve gets so tight she can't roll it anymore, so she shoves it up to my shoulder where it sits tight around my arm.

She says, Sailors refer to it as Angel Stern, Navigatoria, and sometimes the Star of Arcady. Regardless, it's the end of the Little Dipper; follow it from there. The Little Dipper is not a constellation but an asterism, which is a distinctive group of stars. The constellation is Ursa Minor: Little Bear. The cup of the dipper is the bear's flank; its tail is the handle.

She tells me, Recline your seat more. I do and the seat falls back until I'm almost prone. She wraps her arms around my exposed arm in a tight hug so that my arm has very little mobility. Exactly halfway up my bicep she bites me again, a deep, full bite as if she were eating some tough food that needed sharp incisors. I wince then buck in the chair, but she has my arm so tight that her teeth don't lose their grip. Pain comes in glittering waves like sunlight through water and blurs everything.

Above, the Seven Sisters of the Little Dipper twinkle back at me, spinning out from the North Star. After she lets go Tina says,

Polaris is constant; if you were at the North Pole it'd be directly overhead, but in 14,000 years—because the earth wobbles so much—Vega will become the North Star.

Nietzsche says, As long as you still experience the stars as something "above you" you lack the eye of knowledge.

Tina sits back up. I start to follow her but she says to me, Please don't do that I prefer you reclining, and so I sink back down. From somewhere on her clothes she extracts a safety pin, and I can see her bending it so that the clasp, the safety part of the pin, is bent out of the way of the needle. I expect it to glisten with light but since there's very little light out here it's just a black line, like a scratch on film. Everything looks different in the dark.

The bite starts to register fully in my head and there's so much pain I can't think of any words. Memories flash on my eyes the way the sun leaves afterimages when you look away. The pain opens up doors and behind the doors are things Tina and I have been trying to forget so we can be happy.

I say, Once we knew a girl who was your sister and she left on a plane for New York.

She says, I don't want to talk about it.

Watch these two planets spread one degree farther apart with each passing day.

Tina says, Of the seven stars in Ursa Minor, only five of them are named. Polaris and Kocab and Pherkad and Yildun and Pherkad Minor, but the other two, for whatever reason, don't have names. Polaris has thirteen names but two of her sisters have none. Please make a fist.

I make a fist and in the little light there is that we slowly become accustomed to I can see a few meager veins extrude from my flesh. When I make a fist my wrist hurts from the crescent bruises she's left. I want to talk about her sister who left on a plane for New York but I don't know how.

We haven't talked about it since she left. If I look at Tina her eyes say, It happened; nothing more. What we did to her has no names yet.

I say, Do you miss her?

Tina replies, I loved her very much, and then the needle is suddenly very close.

When I open my mouth again to speak, she puts a finger to it to silence me, so that the line of my slightly open lips forms a cross with her finger. Shhhh, she tells me. I hear her smile. With her right hand her fingers encircle my wrist around the bruise she left, and with the needle in the other hand, she begins to lightly dot my veins with it.

Betelgeuse, Procyon and the brilliant twinkling Sirius, the 'Dog Star' 36 degrees to Moon's lower right, form the nearly equilateral Winter Triangle.

Once she is sure I won't relax my fist and she won't lose the veins, she releases her grip and rests her hand on my groin while she continues to prick the skin, deeper each time.

Nietzsche says, The degree and kind of a man's sexuality reach up into the ultimate pinnacle of his spirit.

My eyes start tracing Ursa Minor so I don't think about the pain. Tracing is the verb and Ursa the noun and Minor the adjective but tracing Ursa Minor is one action that flows smoothly between my eyes and the points of light in the sky so that my head dissolves into the stars and the only thing left is her hand and her needle against my body.

Sometimes you run your hands over the same length of my skin, over and over, until it irritates, over and over until it hurts. When I am with you, my body decays. So I rake my fingers against your back and your breasts until you gasp. Perhaps I do this because cutting into your body allows me to feel safe about my own, but I doubt this very much.

There are moments during intercourse with you that my body divides in two, and my head flies on an airplane in the stars while my body parts are fucking you.

You are on top of me, turned around and I'm sitting up so that I can reach around to stroke you, and in the absence of your face, your back and arms and legs dissolve into a pure nudity. Pornographic or erotic or asexual, without your face this borders on an intense masturbation. My head is on a plane, flying to New York like your sister did, you have no head and your hands run the length of my thighs over and over until it hurts while black blood flows out in jet streams from your truncated head.

Perhaps you are right; perhaps a kiss is just a kiss.

Outside people watch us and the vultures and jackals gather and tear these people from limb to limb and carve out chunks of flesh from their naked, waiting bodies.

For the Hindus, Kama who is Desire is male and Rati who is Pleasure is female. With you sometimes I wonder who is who and which is which.

You could be Babylon and she could be Zion, and I could have hung my harps on your willows. You could be Jupiter and she Venus, you could be moving apart at the rate of one degree a night; you could have any name but your own. You could have the thirteen names of Sirius, and Betelgeuse and I could watch you from our near-60 degree angles, so long as we lose these names. It's the only chance we have left.

I'm fighting to stay conscious but the alternation of her boring into my veins and kneading my cock makes it difficult and I keep blacking out. There's barely enough space in the car to breathe and all I can see are the stars through the moonroof, a small and strange light. I say, You and your sister were very close, weren't you?

We're only two years apart, born in the same month which is Gemini. You still want her don't you?

Tonight brilliant Venus is just over 2 degrees above Jupiter, in WSW to W at dusk. Watch these two planets spread one degree farther apart with each passing day.

The needle goes in and out my arm, slick with blood. I float up out through the moonroof into the stars of Ursa Minor. Two of the stars are unnamed thus untamed and wild and I float between them, unsure, my breathing shallow and my penis rock hard. She carefully undoes the zipper with one hand, takes out my cock and encircles it with her fingers.

Please stop, I say. I love you and we're happy.

Nietzsche says, The enormous expectation in sexual love and the sense of shame in this expectation spoils all perspective for women from the start.

The Bible says I should let my right hand wither and my tongue cleave to the roof of my mouth if I do not hold Jerusalem above my highest joy.

Tina says, I miss her a lot.

I am water.

The Moon is in ESE to SE, with the Gemini twins, Castor above Pollux, to the Moon's left, and Procyon below the Moon.

She lets go of my penis and pulls out the needle from me and sits up in her chair. What no one seems to understand is that it isn't names that are important but relationships, the distance between objects.

Tina says, I have to talk to you. Because you don't know.

I can barely breathe, my skin is cooling as the air dries the blood that trickles out and I almost faint again. I am water.

Tina says, I want to tell you about the first time I had sex.

Tina says, George Mühleck leaves a copier open all night long under the stars and it produces a black piece of paper which he entitles *Copy of the Stars.* You see me and you even talk about me, but I'll always escape and then I'm on a plane to New York. There are no names for me yet.

Tina says, Once there was a man between her and I. We were young. He wanted her more than he wanted me. I had only one option, as far as I was concerned. So I fucked him. Because she wouldn't.

There are splotches in my vision. Big bursts of light and a strange buzzing noise in my head. My mouth is dry and I can taste the air inside it and can smell the drop of semen clinging to the end of my penis. My balls and my arm ache. I am fluid, liquid.

Tina says, That was the first time I had sex. Sex had been built up so much by that point. Because I was young. Because I was a girl.

There you have it: the splotches of light, the buzzing sound, the aching in my body, the sweet iron smell of come and blood, the dead taste of air. All five senses reminding me I'm about to pass out. All five senses telling me I'm water.

Tina says, The first time I had sex I didn't even know it was happening. There aren't any trumpets. Not even immense pain or a torrent of blood. It was just there, and then it was over. And he was asleep.

Slowly, feeling comes back into my body, my breathing slows down, my erection fails, and I begin to think straight again. I say, What about your sister.

Tina says, You remember how sometimes she and I went out and she didn't want to drink so she'd let me use her I.D. And I, to make things fair, gave her mine. And as a joke, I sometimes called her Tina. But long before that, before I went to college, when I was first learning about astronomy, I told her about Castor and Pollux, the Gemini Twins. And she asked me if she was Pollux or Castor and I said it didn't matter, together we were Gemini. So the last time I saw her, at the airport, she was about to board and she turned and started to cry, we both were crying, and I told her, No matter what happens, we would always be Gemini; Castor and Pollux, and she would always know where to find me if she needed me.

I say to her, You were telling me about sex.

Tina says, The important thing is that sex is never as good as you think it should be. The important thing is that you always come back for more.

Just as I'm recovering, Tina sticks her index finger and thumb into her mouth to wet them, and then circles my cock again, moving her hand up and down.

Do you have a name for it? she asks.

Like a proper name? Like Henry?

No, just a name, she says.

I have always liked cock.

She says, I think I prefer penis. Cock is vulgar. Penis is slightly immature. Vagina isn't like that; why is that?

I open my mouth but she says, When we're children, before you know about sex, vagina is like that. Before sex there is only the vagina and the penis and they are strangers, and of course when you are young, there are no other words for it. Sex changes that.

I want to ask her why the simple words, like yellow, have so many synonyms, but according to the Thesarus penis and vagina have only a few, and I want to ask her why there is no other word for sister, or for love, but I don't ask her any of this.

Instead I try to say, It isn't the names that are important—but after the word It, she says, Maybe because penis is a thing, whereas I have only the absence of a thing. A penis sticks out, intrudes; you can be aware of its presence without understanding it because it's just there. By the time a man knows a vagina, he either controls it or it controls him.

She says, Will you take me out here again tomorrow night?

I begin to think about how I'll look tomorrow morning, in daylight. I start wondering what colors the bruises will be.

Yes, I tell her. Then I say, You and your sister are both very beautiful.

She asks me, her mouth in the dark smiling with what could bitterness or love she asks me, Why don't you ever say her name?

Then she leans her head over; the penis disappears inside her.

*

From Abrams Planetarium Skywatcher's Diary; Friday, February 26th: *Moon is in ESE at dusk. Pollux and Castor, the Gemini twins, are about 11 and 15 degrees to Moon's upper left. Procyon is 14 degrees to Moon's lower right. Sirius, brightest nighttime star, is 26 degrees lower right of Procyon. Even brighter than Sirius, the planets Venus and Jupiter are just over 3 degrees apart in WSW to W.*

Once there were two women.

I imagine two fish, circling in the water, darting towards and away from each other. Desire has two terms, the subject and object, but as the two fish flutter towards each other, trying to come together, the water itself becomes a third term, the water which is the medium.

The subject who desires, and the object of desire. No. It is rather this: the one who desires, the one desired, and Desire itself.

Together we are seeking her sister. Her beautiful sister. Seeking, the verb, sister, the noun, beautiful, the adjective. No, it is rather this: seeking her beautiful sister, dissolving into one action, one movement, flowing like water, without words or names, two stars floating in the sky which is the sea which is water which is Desire and Pleasure, masculine and feminine, eating and eaten, all together like water.

Once I knew two women. They were sisters.

properties of language
DAVID SHIELDS

My blood pressure zoomed to 150/100. Rachel suggested that I try Transcendental Meditation. She'd abandoned it long ago, after only a few months, but it had helped her stop smoking so much pot. At my TM initiation ceremony, I was informed that "Sho-ring" was my mantra. After a few days, I told my TM teacher I couldn't use "Sho-ring" because every time I said it out loud, all it signified to me was how to perform a marriage proposal. I asked for another mantra. The teacher said no.

*

My first name is "David," which means "beloved." My last name is "Shields" (originally "Shildkraut" until my father changed it after the war). My fate is inscribed in my name: out of who knows what fear, I shield myself from my beloved. A more optimistic interpretation would, of course, see my name indicating that I shield my beloved, or that my beloved shields me, but part of the problem is that such glosses seem to me too glossy.

*

A student in my class, feeling self-conscious about being much older than the other students, told me that he had been in prison. I asked him what crime he had commited, and he said, "Shot a dude." He wrote a series of very good but very stoic stories about prison life, and when I asked him why the stories were so tight-lipped, he explained to me the jailhouse concept of "doing your own time," which means that when you're a prisoner, you're expected not to burden other prisoners by complaining about your incarceration, or regretting what you had done, or especially, claiming you hadn't done it. "Do your own time"—it's a seductive slogan. I find that I quote it to myself frequently, but really I don't believe in it at all. We're not, after all, in prison. Stoicism bores me. What I ultimately believe in is talking about everything until you're blue in the face.

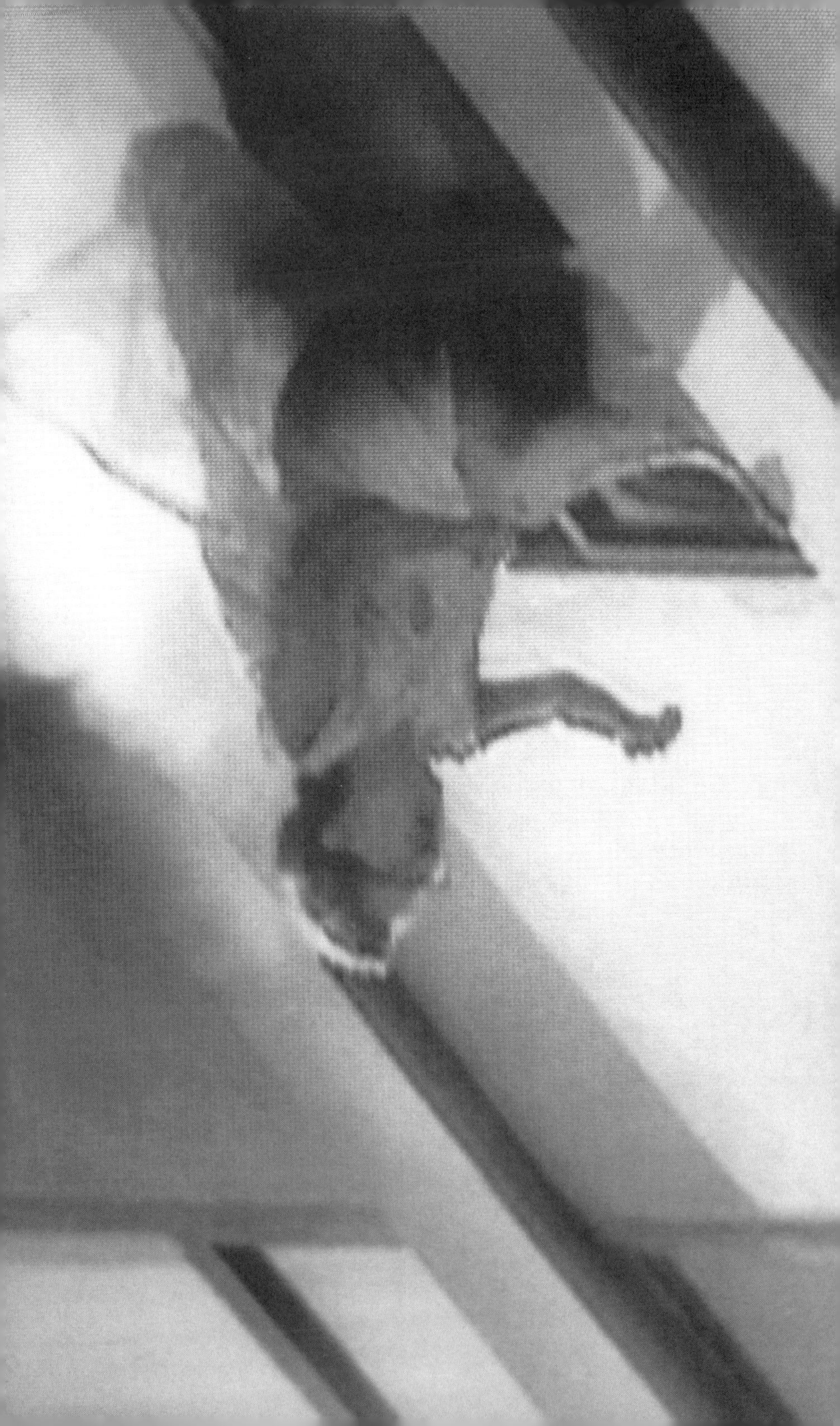

It was not for her to decide.

when good people do bad things

THE LA PUSH, WA
EXPERIMENTAL
WRITING & TYPING CLUB

The ferry boat horn blew, shaking Pinkie awake from her brief stupor. Before her, before the little party of friends all clad in yellow blazers and their trademark lime-green scarves, the gray waters of the bay spread out like so much curdled milk, all wrinkly and clotted, worried by the fresh winds of a late-fall shower.

"My coffee's cold," Pinkie complained, swirling the cloudy brew about in its soggy cup. "Are we almost there yet, or what?" Pinkie was a sugary little tart, 6'3" in her wellies, and with a personality to match. Naturally, as with ducklings following a much larger duck or bird, the little group of friends swirled like cloudy coffee in the wake of a tempestuous Pinkie.

"Almost, Pinkie," tiny Stallion murmured. And despite his diminuitive stature he seemed to grow in size until his presence could be felt on the other side of the Pacific Rim—and grew still further, kept growing in fact until he had achieved almost mythic proportions. We were mesmerized, our small band of outsiders, topside on that ferry racing into the mists of oblivion, it seemed we were everywhere at once and yet so randomly dispersed as to be almost general. But I stray.

After the man had sent himself over the edge. After the fire and the rain. After the mountain had ventured in her heaven skirt toward the boat and retreated in her bustle and rapture. Etc. After that we arrived in WindSlow. The Part of the Harbor where the indelicacy of traveling packed like sardines, where the vivid memories of the corn dogs and chowder were as dust. In short, we debarked. Or were debarked. We were sent out of the boat by the nasty man in his outfit. We were sent away for what Misty did. She may or may not have done it. I mean Mars says she didn't and Stallion wasn't looking and it had to do with cheese.

We thrust deeply into the valley of the Cheesewallop that night—the mist was close; a near mist. We crossed and uncrossed the Don. The night wore on. The air became thicker as Pinkie was laid low by the oppressiveness. And still it squalled. Wine flowed that night in a stream rain. The stallion rose to the barometer again and it fell further still as we fell, into the mist, the rain, the dark night of the Sol Duc. My thoughts were dragged back to Italy, O Sole Duce. . . ill Duce. . . my heart ached for Pinkie as she wallowed in her bath of pain, the pain. And the fromage.

Pony wilted while Stallion rose and plumbed the depths of the perimeter. We have to assume he found release. Mars finally got past halfway. Which was a relief to him, a horse like that needs a big corral.

In Cheesewhallop the trees were not all soft and expected. No some of them were hard and deciduous. In fact, they were found to be 'fucking deciduous' by some reports. Back in France most things were soft and expected. Or at the very least, warm. The keyboards there were all very different. Butt Butt Butt Butt Butt Butt Butt Butt Butt Butt Butt Butt Butt Butt Butt Butt Butt Butt Butt Butt Butt Butt Butt Butt Butt Butt Butt Butt Butt Butt Butt Butt Butt Butt Butt Butt Butt Butt Butt Butt Butt Butt Butt Butt Butt Butt Butt Butt Butt Butt Butt Butt Butt Butt Butt Butt Butt Butt Licker licker licker licker licker licker licker licker licker.

The man finally left in the afternoon just before tea. I was exhausted. I would have to say that because so much of translation is physical, I strained some inexplicable bones. In fact, I would have to say that language is rooted in the physical. In cheese, in bread, in the valley and all these knives.

Because we had crossed over so many rivers, we were changed less and so passed from the specific to the general. The Pacific, the realm of the General, the crusty old salt, an equivocating buttsucker whose years of living on rations of corn and saltpork had so corrupted his questionable virtue as to render him thin-assed butt-ugly slab-sided ditch built buggers, he thought. DAMN THEIR HAWSE-HOLES! But he was cool as a cucumber butt inside. I'll starve them out, by god, he reasoned. And with that, he was a new stallion. No longer uncertain, fearful of the talk in the admiralty generations ahead. They're not here now, he reasoned. The buttholes, he added. The dolphins playing in the wake seemed to echo his sentimentalism. Can dolphins think? he reasoned. Why do I torment myself so? he reasoned.

He was less than a stallion but more than a mule, at least in the way he ate. I first met him in a restaurant near Blin. We shared clams and a beer and he told me about Spain. Spain bored me. I told him about marlins, the way the fish arches when you spear yourself, naked as a fig, beneath the sheets, with the fish. He was a stallion, or less. He mewed like a fish when I pierced him beneath the sheets. He shared clams near Blin with a mule. I was fishing from a pier when I saw him, shit-faced and mewling. I mauled the clammy stallion with a spear, bored of Spain.

stopping time

MICHAEL KROETCH

141

—

A true story.

IT WAS NOT CONVENIENT.

HE LOOKED EXACTLY SIMILAR TO THE WAY THEY LOOKED.

Same clothes, same language, same laughter, same kind of skin.

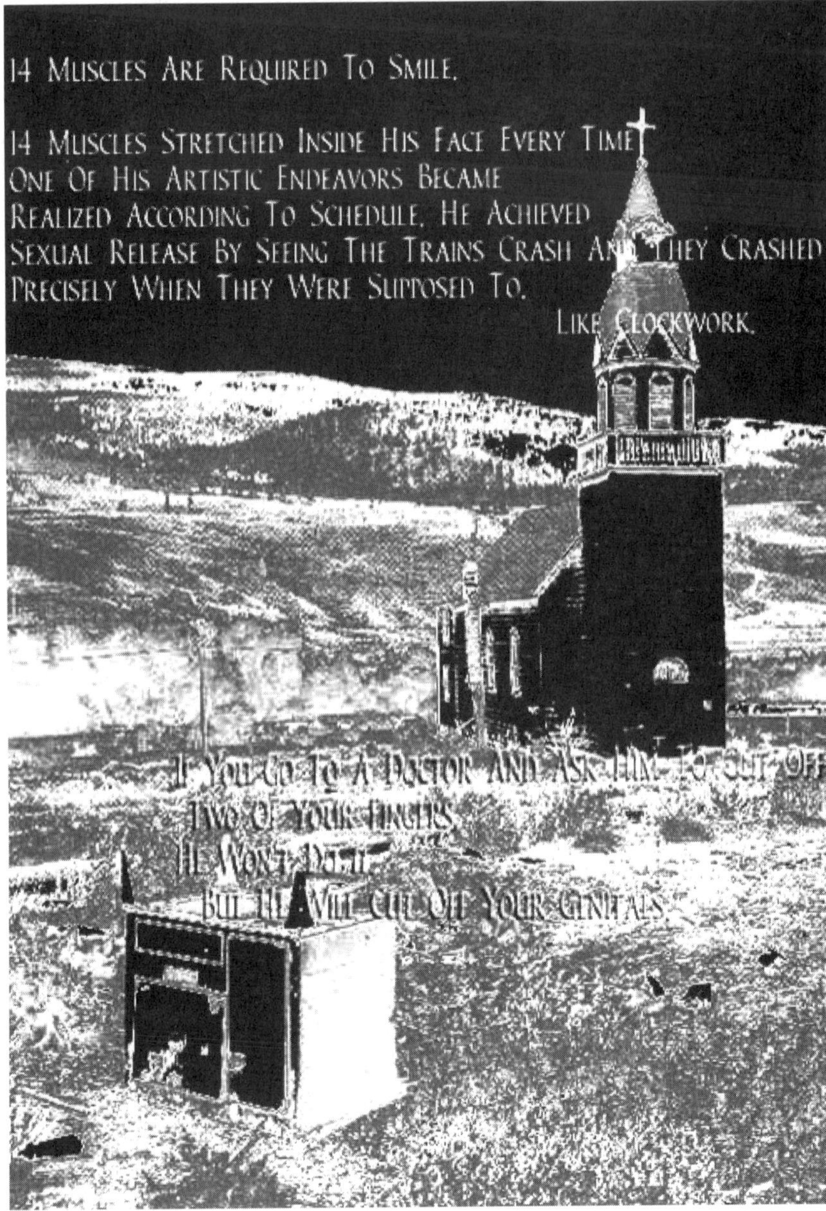
14 Muscles Are Required To Smile.
14 Muscles Stretched Inside His Face Every Time
One Of His Artistic Endeavors Became
Realized According To Schedule. He Achieved
Sexual Release By Seeing The Trains Crash And They Crashed
Precisely When They Were Supposed To.
Like Clockwork.
If You Go To A Doctor And Ask Him To Cut Off
Two Of Your Fingers,
He Won't Do It
But He Will Cut Off Your Genitals.

He had been standing right in front of them the whole time.

HE SAID
IN THAT
MOMENT
WHEN
THAT
BAT
WAS IN
HIS
HAND
IT
FELT
LIKE HE
WAS
STOPPING
TIME
ITSELF.

They had very strict rules. They had a very clear code of behavior. They needed order and discipline and people who were able to translate abstract data into well-regulated rhythm. They needed people who could repeat the same activity over and over again without error. They needed a firm hand to guide the controls of their machines. Efficiency was the bottom line. They worshipped it.

He said he was hollow inside.

Like a TV.

He wiped his sperm off
his hands with a napkin
from a fast food
restaurant.

His notebooks held a careful record of future crashes.

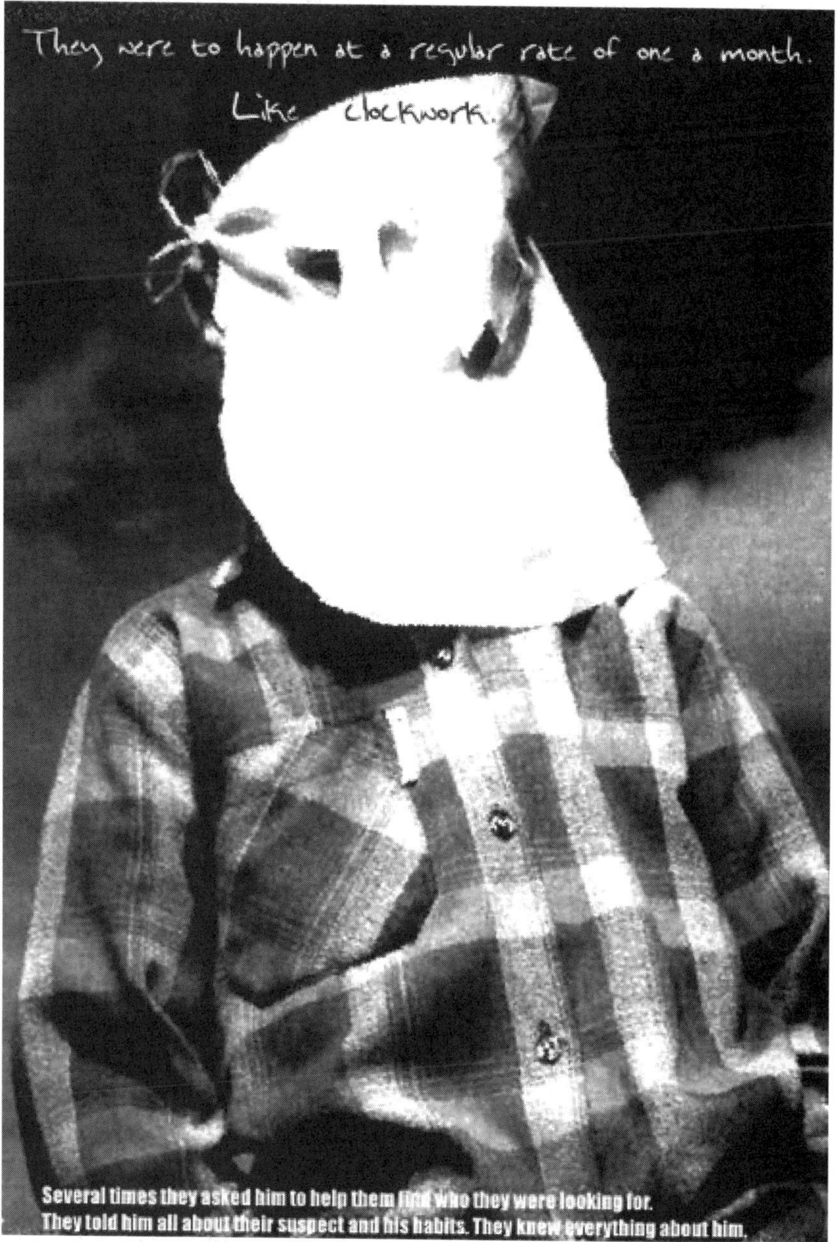

Except what he looked like.

BRIAN CHRISTOPHER

old school

Tanner thawed. He coughed and breathed, kneading his hands, the meat of them, as the fire hissed and spit, lifting steam.

"Dead right," he said, and kicked at the wood.

The body, to his back, mouthed air, and the bullet, deep in the body's flesh, in the dark red muscle, cooled.

On the roof, snow shifted, startling Tanner where he stood.

"Shouldn't have come is all," he said over his shoulder, feet stomping blood. "Shouldn't, I'm saying. But who'll listen."

Turning then, Tanner hitched at the belt, worked holster back to hip. He fingered leafy brown from pocket into cheek, bit and sprayed, walked to the body, not looking.

Head cocked, he, Tanner, strained for sirens.

None.

Wind only, trees, ice.

Again, face to body, he locked eye to frozen eye with it, eased hand to gun, drew and aimed, triggered the steel.

Roof snow slid as the body pitched, settled.

"Bastard," Tanner muttered. "There's the lesson."

the wait

The finger went in easy. The slick length of it disappeared into the opening.

Fetter felt nothing. He turned it, slowly, withdrew.

The sound was like kissing.

He tried two, faster, straight to knuckles.

Then three.

Then the hand, thumb pressing palm.

Nothing, still.

Fetter lay back, looked up into spiny leaves, the thick green of them. Inhaling pine, he closed his eyes, tried to roll. He braced, wished, hoped, imagined the sound of it, the shifting organs, view.

Then he relaxed, rested. His eyes opened to the same green, waving, breezy, mocking.

He remembered the stiff feel of branches as he climbed, the sticky pitch on skin, the tickle.

Fetter looked again at the opening, its tangle, its rich red oozing. He watched the finger slip inside, then out. He repeated it, waited.

evidence

It was all I could do in the dark with the little light and the blisters. It was all I could do. But I won't go back. It's bad luck going back. I probably should, now that it's rained and the ground has softened some. I should drop it down a few more feet, go at the same hole with fresh hands. It's just not deep enough. I wonder if it's ever deep enough.

If only I'd buried it further down in the first place. The body, I mean, not the gun. The gun's just fine in the river, in the channel, deep. I'm not worried about the gun. But the body. . . I just can't stop thinking about how the ground was that night, and how I couldn't hardly see for digging. And then the shovel, the blisters; I just couldn't dig no more. Pulling the trigger didn't bring no blisters. Or loading the body into the trunk. But the digging. . . I just couldn't.

You know, I don't so much mind talking about the burying part, but don't ask me about the killing, the way that bastard wouldn't keep it shut. I must have told him a half dozen times to keep his drunk mouth tight, but he wouldn't do it. Just kept pushing that way, drinking and talking, not letting it alone.

So that's that, and now he's down with the worms, if they can even get to him though that hard ground. I ought to go up there, just to make sure no animals have dug at the grave, just to see. I could be real careful, pretending to hunt. That would do it, sure enough. But then, my only gun is gone, underwater, below the bridge. I shouldn't tell you which one, but I guess it wouldn't matter. It's long gone by now. They'd never drag the river just to get at a gun that might or might not be there. They wouldn't drag it, would they? I don't think they would. But they might make me take that serum so I'd tell them where the gun and the body are. Could they do that? Make me take the serum?

Wait. What am I saying? Even if they're watching, even if they suspect, they're not gonna catch me. Because I won't go up there. Not for nothing. I won't do it. Not until after it rains again, anyway. And in the dark, with better light, so I can be sure to get at the dirt easier.

Yeah, that's it. Maybe. After it rains.

listening to mainie jellett

ELIZABETH SHÉ

When Mary was raped and the resulting child, her son,
proclaimed The Savior, anger filled her
bleached her skin white, her eyes blue
Rage blew out the top of her head, erupted into a halo
of pure energy
She was pronounced A Saint.

another mistranslation

"Surely you're joking, Mr. Firebrand. You're not seriously thinking of transposing X to Y!" He stared at me while I scribbled and rescribbled the equation.

x + y - mz/22 || aby/12 = 14e

Could it be correct? Could this really be the formula I'd been working to perfect my entire lifespan of eight and sixty years? I checked and cross-checked, pulling first Einstein, then Hawking, then Lamarr closer. I used the Chudnovskys' pi, trusting my Russian forebears' intuition in all things numerical.

x - y + mz/22   or was it 23?

I was so close, so close!

I beat my head on the table in frustration. Drops of blood smeared on the pages of my algorithm notebook.

I looked, then looked again, not believing my eyes.

"The blood!" I cried, pointing to the paper so even Marcowicz would see. "Look!" The blood, my beautiful blood, had completed the equation, had changed the *y* to *x*, the *e* to *0*.

x + y - mz/22 || abx/12 = 140

I had found it – the secret formula men had craved, desired and searched for since the dawn of Timex.

I looked up at Marcowicz, grinning like Dostoevsky's Idiot. "We're rich, man. Rich!

The walls are not yet cool enough to touch.

It wasn't as if he never looked back.

crossing the marimba

SHAMINA SENARATNE

Crossing a marimba—
wooden bridge over a woman's silvery hair, hair flowing lush,
curly over smooth round tummies, larger and small fertility
stones, salmon fingerlings sheltering in their shadows—crossing
the marimba wooden bridge over the frothy sound of static
bubbling behind double-paned glass, I am slowed by blue
flickering light thrown up in fragments from the river bed and
my ribs sound the song of my footsteps.

Running along the green bottle bank feeling the humidity of
spray on the tips of the fingers of my left hand, effervescence
escaping her slender sides, expanding her journey, softening my
hair into curls near my face—running along the greenbottlebank
over moss and new leaves sprouting, I follow her glistering,
blinking, winking, water tumbling pop-topsey,
toward the inlet's still grace.

*

Crossing the marimba, *remember?*
wooden bridge over a woman's silvery hair, hair falling lush,
curly over smooth round tummies, *Tea cup to the rim* larger
and small fertility stones *when your water broke? don't spill*
salmon fingerlings sheltering
baby soft and warm, my new milk dribbling down her chin,
crossing the marimba wooden bridge *Mamma made me*
hot chocolate, creamy over the frothy *Foam soft*
against the back of my throat, tongue bubbling behind double

paned glass, *swimming, floating in warm liquid* I am
aware of blue flickering *television hissing in the corner at 4*
a.m. light thrown up in fragments from the river bed, and my
ribs sound the song of my footsteps.

Running along the green bottle bank
feeling the humidity of spray *time for bath baby*
a baby bath, baby on the tips *aren't you sweet?*
on the fingers of my left hand, *aren't you sweet, hmmm*
effervescence caressing her slender sides, a blanket for her journey
yes, aren't you sweet, hmmm? softening my thoughts into curls
near her face, running along the greenbottlebank over moss and
new leaves sprouting, I follow her blinking, winking water,
tumbling topsey *you're my darling, yes you are* toward the
the inlet's still. . .

*

Crossing the marimba wooden bridge
over the frothy sound of static *I met him in a jazz bar of all things.*
He was dark and interesting bubbling behind double paned glass,
I was aware of blue flickering *and I felt rich*
and colourful. I bought him a fizzy drink, and told him my life
story, light released in fragments from the river bed *how I lived*
as a stream and would someday reach the sea. *He asked if I*
still would be happy then—lost in a large body of water,
thing of beauty that I was, and my ribs! *His eyes were lit with a*
boy's mischief and sound *I laughed inside and out and told*
him the song of my footsteps. *I intended to become lost in*
beauty.

Crossing the marimba over a woman's silvery voice,
he was amused rushing lush, curly over smooth round tummies,
and allowed his beauty to accompany mine. larger and small
fertility stones, salmon fingerlings sheltering in their shadows,
For years we have travelled within the humidity of
spring's effervescence *over gravel beds and smooth stones,*
lingered around fallen trees, fallen through stone throats

escaping her slender sides, *our tongues against the canyon*
walls, expanding her journey *tasting each sand grain passing,*
each passing place tasted, and let go, softening my hair
into curls near my face—running along the greenbottlebank
yesterday I noticed he wasn't with me
over moss and new leaves sprouting *perhaps he has gone*
ahead, but his beauty is still   I follow her glistering,
blinking winking water tumbling

*

Crossing the marimba wooden bridge over the hush, lush, *early*
Saturday morning, I am aware of blue flickering over the frothy
sound of static *while our children sit in cartoon* bubbling
behind double paned glass *bliss,*   *my husband and I slip into the*
shower and I am aware of blue flickering   *soap bubbles slide*
over his shoulder to my arm, from his chest to my smooth round
tummy, larger and smaller   light released in fragments to
to the river bed *fertility stone, salmon fingerling sheltering in our*
shadows and my ribs sound the song of my footsteps.

Swimming along the green bottle bank,
feeling the humidity of spray softening my hair
into curls near my face   effervescence settling over moss and
new leaves sprouting,   I am glimmering, blinking winking
water,   tumbling toward the inlet's embrace.

restraining order

DOUG NUFER

16
Epilogue

So we finally abandoned the tabloid world, those madmen and deadlines reverberating throughout the raw, devastated corridors of soiled inspiration where order restrains the soul.

To say it's entirely over would be insidious, for death happens and we endure. Certainly careers come and go. And I keep more than the terrifying memory of pulp fiction made fact. In truth, I embrace a clean feeling of satisfaction to understand that moments, in and of themselves, are real materializations of life itself. Much as I rue the impression that I am running away, the conviction that I have made my own vitality cheers me as I prepare to move to The Island.

Brad and I will make our peace doing what folks must do to live life to the hilt. Raise a family? I don't know.

But I do know I will continue to struggle to conceive a reality of truth, beauty, and trust. And no amount of content providing, poetry, freelance contracting, or memoir recreation may synthesize what has been irreconcilably ruptured. But I go on.

1
Prologue

Many readers believe, I suppose, that it's conspicuously self-indulgent for authors' acknowledgments to ramble before their stories or ideas open. So to be brief, the reason for writing an account like this is to have a say. Even editors or publishers, with their concern limited by commerce, contribute to an essential empowerment of self-expression.

My former co-workers, who risked their lives toiling in the worst circumstances, deserve my undying gratitude.

My friends, who took my frantic pleas, panic attacks, and sobbing calls, surely merit some kind of sainthood.

My readers: I mean the ones other than the imbeciles who sought their two-bit fortunes in the horoscope, who delved through to the essence of what I meant, warrant a special place in my Pantheon.

My husband Brad, who suffered all this and more indignities than anyone ought withstand, I have first, last, and forever loved, honored, attended, and above all gratified with every last word indeed.

2
Nobody's Dream Job

Talk about lost illusion. To be the editor of *Spicy Bits*? It was just a lousy scandal sheet, nationally infamous for bad taste, bad prose, obscenely high salaries, and a certain knack for catapulting its staff to literary glory and prestige once their tours of duty ended and offers for book contracts lured muckrackers from the scum of their own creation. This career move appealed to me, odd as it was, although I knew that the editor would bait every drooling slob who took *Spicy Bits* to heart. In hand, I'd have the opportunity of a lifetime or *Life, Time,* and *Spicy Bits,* as Kenner Vanderbilt liked to say. Kenner, a black sheep of a family of great publishers, rich kid grown bored with pure leisure, an all-round romantic who never lost sight of the bottom line or hem line or every skirt in his office. He even called us that. For Kenner, life was a game of sins and skirts: "The higher the better, fire the pants," was his way of acting suave.

Insane, I told myself. All I had to do was stick it out for a year or so. I only had to survive.

15
Shot to Hell

"Jesus Christ," said my cop savior, sopping sweat and tears in the bloody aftermath of the wounded and the dead.

But it was obvious what he meant, looking around the office that became a battlefield: chickens came home to roost. Violence at Work, sexy subject as it was, came under heavy fire from police groups for its lurid, realistic advice: how to murder your boss, co-workers, and anyone else in the way.

"Vietnam or more like Cambodia," he said, slowly slipping his hot, spent revolver into a rather feminine patent leather holster.

"Nice shot, big boy," I quipped. What's the proper accolade when someone saves your ass? My hands were shaking so much I lit my nose rather than the cigarette dangling from my twitching lips, lips so grateful for one more sweet kiss of breath.

"Amazing," said the cop, "he came at you," flicking his Zippo, "but suddenly froze," as the dynamic guerilla reporter who'd been Buster Penn oozed harmlessly at our feet.

"Fuck," said the cop. "How'd you—"

I said, "Want it dead or alive?"

14
Filing on Deadline

Peen always made deadline, so we thought
he'd be in that day to deliver in person. As
my neck stuck out for the chopping, I kept
trying his line, so when the ruckus started,
I was more angry at not getting through to
those who owed me copy than at whatever
crisis they thought they were having. This
commotion seemed to be the equivalent of
any other Friday at the office: shrieking to
escape from the pressure of the deadline or
release this impossible tension before they
exploded. Little did I know.
To the desk holes and closets, the staffers
plunged to duck the potshots of the writer
gone wacko, that strung-out stringer, who
once wrote but now was Police Beat meat.
Why didn't we issue the restraining order,
like our attorney said? But just as we had
documented in the domestic killer series,
restraining orders did nothing but provoke
the bastard.
Kicking in the door, he stood in a haze of
rage. Reeking with a musk stench of bear
grease, he took the Uzi and unzipped his
pants while I popped the weasel question.

3
Like an Old Pro

He wore army fatigues and shaved his head.
It seemed like a costume. His specialty was
undercover. That's what he told me at first;
I had no reason not to believe him.
Most of the others, plugged fanatically into
their computers, were too busy to give me a
clue of how to settle into the high-pressure
routines trapping them like rats trapped in
a maze they somehow had set themselves to
escape from. The ludicrous scene, with all
jabbering and hollering, strangely soothed
Buster Peen. Generously, he introduced me
to everyone, as if he—not the publisher—
had to make me feel at home.
Charmed by his gentle and tender manner,
I told him to do what he wanted, not asking
what he had in mind or what he had done.
More amused than aggravated by the man
calling me Sweets, I must have blushed as
he took my hand.
"But I warn you, Sweets, I stop at nothing.
A caged wild boar in the rut doesn't know
desire or the frustration I have known. I'm
hard on folks. Maybe sometimes someone
gets hurt? A reporter has no friends."

4
Crocodile Tear Sheets

If a reporter has no friends, an editor has swarms of coy enemies who pretend to be intimate or madly in love with her. I soon maneuvered to brush off the creeps and get what I wanted from those who'd give it to me; if their feelings got hurt or if they got bloated with endearment from a remark I made, so much the better. Most of my job threatened to become a psychological war exercise, where I couldn't drop my guard for a moment. Although Peen helped me, something told me that this was the worst attack of all, relentlessly ongoing, a duel to the death.

Invited out to lunch to discuss story ideas, I found myself with him in some nook at Pinkie's Hideaway, arguing date rape and how women wanted it more than men, and they wanted rough sex, putting up a fight, so when the men fought to break through, the orgasms were mind-boggling. As if it was only part of his proposal, he squeezed my thigh.

Only a squeeze it was, just so the obscene thought sank in.

13
Restraining Order

A sick joke or the coda to a series that got out of hand? If only it were that obvious. Committed to space constraints, we were forced into running every damn word of the violence at work series. And, true to his word, the ace reporter without friends stopped at nothing to pillage the topic. I couldn't believe some of the wacky ploys Peen resorted to as he shoved himself in as far as he could go.

Of course, he had to take the arch role of disgruntled employee. And of course, this made him look silly.

People thought he was a riot. And so they teased him. "Yo, Psycho, cock your gun," a rub of the crotch and a wink were their milder taunts. I tried to make them stop; then everyone would go off another way. Insisting it was part of the whole routine, they'd say this was a game to ease tension. The game would resume, and therefore it festered until it was worst than before. So to keep everyone in line, legal aimed to hit Peen with a restraining order. Not that any saw this as a restraint. It was insurance.

12
Corporate Lie Ability

Because of some of the outrageous claims *Spicy Bits* made, people felt we often got sued or at least threatened by legal action. Actually, ridiculous as it might be to aver, unbelievable as it might be to accept, this never happened simply because our files sizzled with all kinds of hot spicy bits on otherwise squeaky clean, fine, and honest citizens. But much of this stuff we never used since it was of no interest to anyone other than those who might have sued us for saying anything offensive about them. You had to do retractions, of course, and this, paradoxically, served to provide us the excuse to print the most disreputable hearsay on the beautiful and the damned, even on the philanthropists who believed they'd never be vilified just for the hell of it, that we would slander them on purpose just because we could.

Our liability insurance lied in retractions. Ironically, then, our lawyer had the worst trouble when it came to dealing with the rude people on our staff. Writers, mostly. They were our biggest liability.

5
Spike of the Devil

Kenner was livid. He burst in raving with a fistful of proof sheets. Enflamed by rage, he demanded why I had spiked the greatest story of the decade, maybe the single most sensational story we ever ran. Usually we worked on three issues and several articles ahead. For various reasons, stories thrived or shriveled up and died. Sure, some were spiked. Others folded by themselves. We dealt with hyperbolically inflated "news" anyway, so I had no idea what he meant.

"You killed date rape. Date rape had all they want, in a word, s-e-x; put them in the driver's seat, identification wise. Or back seat, hubba hubba. Victimizer and victim all in one package."

"To me, it wasn't happening," I said, a la, the story wasn't coming together.

"Come on! Buster has the goods. All the ooze that's shit to print."

I said that was the problem. Peen got in over his head. Besides, it wasn't just a story. It was a power struggle, crude and mean, and if he didn't master that reality, Kenner might as well give up.

6
Lions Head Headlines

"Let me put it this way," I said to Kenner, to put a cap on the date rape veto. "When your underlings get uppity, you put them down, crack the whip, and if that doesn't do the trick, you shoot for the balls."

Kenner shifted nervously. I realized this had to alarm the spoiled brat grown into the man who was my publisher, my boss. Touching his forearm, I said, "But figure some girls, and you know that cheap type: lion hunters. They aim their crack shots at hot men with fame, money, power, or a combo of worthwhile targets plus that essential man quality a girl craves. And those girls aren't what you want. Not as editor. For editor, you get someone into control; not only in control: into it. No lion hunter: a lion tamer."

Kenner, his eyes bright, hard, and dewy, didn't speak but purred into a low growl. Time to change the subject, I thought, not wanting to have to spurn him but needing to set him straight.

"To fit the space, I slash and burn, waste their titles and slap on gory headlines."

11
Kick Back and Backfire

For the first time in weeks, I was free, i.e. going to lunch ceased to require strategy. Over the hump of Peen, I was relieved to put the office back to normal operations, if you ever could have conceived of that *Spicy Bits* office as seeming normal.

On my own at ease and free to kick back, I went to the Hideaway to install myself, roosting in the booth where Peen groped me. I ordered the same drink, noshed on the same swank cheese niblets, dripping creamy goo. I opened a manuscript and, determined to get some light work done, I began to read. But I couldn't see why our articles weren't as fascinating as the queries. The pitch jobs were better than more than half of what was up for the next issue, so I had the perverse desire to do a special edition packed with mail to me since these supplications exemplified the longing to reach some mother or whore in a position to say, yes, you are so good.

I then saw, among the others, the old cut-and-pasted alphabet sort of ransom note, threatening simply to get me.

10
Lose the Loose Cannon

There were seventeen messages blinking from Peen on voice mail, as many e-mails sent and re-sent in variations of the same strident yelps. The ungrateful ace reporter presented a list of silly demands. First off, he wanted to read his copy before printing cast in stone some editorial blunder. Also he wanted final-cut rights, along with the privilege to use his own headlines and subheads. I could suggest but not veto. The cranky, strange, and cumbersome nature of such demands on a weekly paper were, to put it cordially, ridiculous. But not to settle for just this, Peen also craved to be paid more per column inch.

"Kenner, darling," I began, putting on the overdone sweetness to soften him for my retaliation. Unlike Peen's list, mine was condensed to a solitary requirement: one pure vital demand that was absolutely not negotiable.

When I finished, however, he wasn't just backed into a corner; he saw the situation unraveled by itself. Peen was a freelance stringer, i.e. no one you had to fire.

7
Ball Peen Hammer

This moment of discussion with top brass on matters of coping with contributors was rare, if not unprecedented. I handled what needed to be fixed, and our Prince Kenner, King of Clubs, repaired to the golf course because, he said, deals drove from the tee. This simplified my job and gave him what deniability there is in a chain of command. Ordinarily, this suited me fine; at loggerheads with a testy Peen, I wasn't so happy about this arrangement, particularly when Peen made no bones about having to fuck me. Nonetheless, I savored my victory to the extent that it strengthened the position I enjoyed.

Advantages versus disadvantages, it wasn't altogether unheard of to put up with some lunatic if the lunatic did good work. After all, the main reason I gave Peen for killing date rape—and this mattered a lot—the critical period for violence at work was at this very moment, because if he didn't get on it immediately, going postal would go out of fashion. And, I said, stroking his ego, this story he could take all the way.

8
Paste-up Stand-Off

Things moved fast at *Spicy Bits*. But not so fast that someone didn't notice. Close as I was to all that was happening, I went blindly from moment to moment, feeling my way along while keeping reactions to myself. I coped. And when I went home, I unloaded. And Brad, my poor husband, faithful though he was, and I surely was, began to draw the most scandalous conclusions from what he saw as a blatant insecurity on my part. Ridiculous as this is, patterns form so as to appear different to different vantage points.

It was my fear of losing control that had me exerting control, Brad claimed. And this I did, he said, by playing the part of the prick tease.

After setting Brad straight in every way, I got to thinking about how I didn't need that sick job if it was going to demonize me in the eyes of my husband, let alone to make me even begin to feel like a slut for wearing short, tight, and wet-looking leather skirts. Paste 'em up and lay 'em out, I said, set to quit, to rid us of Peen.

9
Centerspread Bingo

A free space, like in Bingo. It happens all the time in layout. So you move it around, plugging the hole, jacking up font size on the pull quotes to modify the way print and images fill the page. There were other slips to watch out for too, such as the quirky unplanned leaps the eye makes from column to column, fusions you didn't ignore, but then prevention of these was necessary.

You had to work harder at averting bad puns and clever secret dirty lines than at interjecting them. And I knew how hard this job of avoiding rude accidents was; that's what I did, at the last moment.

So what went through me in Composing was my fault, even if it wasn't. Anyway, I did it. And everyone knew I did it, and them congratulating me for it even made me feel like a hero. Still, I pondered, for all it accomplished, I couldn't take credit on account of the opportunity made it so blatantly obvious. Like he was preening for a Pulitzer with Bloody Bosses part I, his by-line over a penile enlargement ad.

I have this thing

BILLIE LIVINGSTON

My phone doesn't ring anymore, not the old way. It sounds nothing like a bell now. The new phones gargle—belch when squashed between cushions the way mine is now.

It's my mother. She says, *There's one other thing,* and she pauses as if the aunt-thing, the reason she called two and a half minutes ago was just a ruse, a lead in for something she remained gutless to set free before stuffing the receiver back in its cradle like a sock in its mouth.

I've been thinking, she says, and I remember her old boyfriend who used to say, *Don't think. Please, don't think. I hate to leave you alone for fear you think.*

I've been thinking, she says, *if you should ever find me dead—*

Uck. Must you?

Grow up, it's going to happen sometime. Just listen—she starts to giggle—*Oh shit, why did I start this?*

She clears her throat the way one might place a plush red pillow down for the King's cat. *OK, let's say you come over and find me dead in my bed.*

Sigh. OK, you're dead.

Well, first, you know I take out my partial plate at night and put it beside my bed. On the night table. Right? Well, to begin with, could you put my teeth back in my bloody head. I can't stand the idea of them finding me dead and toothless.

She has this Marilyn Monroe death with beauty fantasy. She pencils on eyebrows every night before bed, with or without company, wanting the cops to hover over her corpse and say, Oh, God, why her? How can the world go on with this lush radiance to light the dawn? She's sixty-three now.

OK, teeth in.

Wait. And also . . . I have this thing . . . well, OK, it's a thing. It's, well . . . when I was going with . . . OK, it's a vibrator. I just don't want . . . if you could make sure that . . .

Oh. Got it. Teeth in, vibrator out.

Ack! Yes. Just put it back in my drawer. No! I mean get rid of it if it's out of my drawer. Or in my drawer. The second drawer from the top. If you could just get rid of it before anyone else comes . . . Oh, Christ. I hope it's you that finds me.

another suitcase story

JUDY MACINNES JR

Symbolism:

If you are given or sold a hot dog, it is a fortunate dream, denoting joy. To sell hot dogs is unlucky; it foretells a great disappointment. To give hot dogs away in a dream is a sure sign of future prosperity.

Characters:

Lucy wrangles those wieners like nobody else. She smells like orangeade: frothy, overly sweet. She wears a pale yellow apron tight around her chest, tied twice around her waist, her yellow (make that, *white*) hair rests on her collarbones. Everything about her is beautiful yellow. Randy wants to tell his wife Janice that he has been in love with Lucy, the cashier at The Drinks & Links, for about eight days now, in love with Lucy and her yellowness. Yesterday, when Lucy silently gave back his change, she gave him a crooked little smile, and he was sure she gave him a little extra relish on his jumbo dog, too.

Protagonist:

Janice rips iceberg lettuce into a small plastic bowl. Her life is ripping apart: Randy hasn't touched her in two weeks and all she can do is eat salad, nothing else will go down. She chops tomatoes into medium sized cubes, the width of thumbs. She met Randy at a "Smokeless Singles Christmas Dance" when he asked her if she wanted to go outside for a cigarette. Eight months later they were married, moved into the basement of her sister's house. Everything was perfect. They were happy. But that was three years ago; now their relationship seems different, and as bitter as the celery she slices. Randy has recently stopped smoking (one of the things they had in common), never talks to her anymore, let alone touch her, and he hasn't been coming home for supper. He usually strolls in after seven.

Dialogue & Conflict:

7:23 P.M. Randy walks in the door.

"Your dinner is cold."

"It's salad for Christ's sake and I've already eaten anyway," Randy says without looking at the set table or his wife. "At the mall," he adds.

"Eating a goddamn hot dog everyday for dinner can't be good for you. You're gonna drop dead if you keep that up."

"I don't want anything else."

"What's wrong with you, Randy? You can tell me. You can talk to me. Why aren't you coming home for dinner anymore?"

Foreshadowing:

The last words spoken from Randy to Janice that night were, "I'm not keen on the salad." He turned on the TV while she wrapped the left-overs in Saran Wrap and cleaned out the kitchen. She threw both the romaine and iceberg lettuce in the garbage, hesitated, and chucked out the bag of sickly white celery as well. 11:30 P.M. Janice reads *Cosmo* in bed while Randy falls asleep on the couch with the TV still on. Janice turns to the contents and scans down the page:

Have You Lost the Will to Date? .... page 50
When You Are Doing Better than He Is .... page 62
I Used to Be a Nun .... page 68
Good News for the Passionate Shopper .... page 78
How to Get the Spice Back into Your Marriage ...... page 88
Does Your Heart Still Belong to Daddy? .... page 89
The Multiple Faces of Guilt .... page 93

She turns to page 88: "How to Get the Spice Back into Your Marriage . . . in Three Easy Steps." On the opposite page there is a luggage ad: a husky man and a petite woman, both in lycra, both holding smiles and suitcases. They are in love. They are about to travel or workout, Janice thinks.

Plot:

1.) Flatter him: tell him he is the best husband in the world. Cook him his favourite dinner.
2.) Surprise him! Answer the door nude or in a sexy blue bra. (Make sure you don't surprise anyone else though—like the telephone repair man!)
3.) Be naughty! Excite him! Be a bad girl!

Setting:

An imitation oak table with four brown vinyl swivel chairs are in the middle of the stage. To the audience's right, a cooking island is positioned. At the end of the island, a telephone sits with a stool beside it. To the left, a buffet stands, displaying Corning Ware. There is a door on each side; the right leading to the other rooms in the basement suite and the left leading outside. The table is fully set: place-mats, napkins folded into tulip shapes, knife, fork, spoon, candles (already lit), a bowl of ripple potato chips centred in the middle of the table, and Janice, seated on the chair facing the stage, feet propped into the air with her thighs leaning on the table. She is wearing g-string panties and his sister's cowboy boots. 7:36 P.M. On the stove, hot dogs are violently boiling and in the oven the buns are being toasted. The phone rings and Janice walks towards the island and swiftly picks up the phone.

Janice: Hello? (urgent) Randy?
Randy: Yeah, it's me. I'm eating out (pauses). . . see ya later. (He hangs up the phone.)

Flashback:

Janice dresses into her jeans and her blue sweater. The blue sweater. Randy gave the sweater to her the first Christmas they spent together; they had only known each other for about a week then. He said it went with her blue eyes and her blue jeans and the blueness of her. Had he forgotten everything? She was going to drive down to that mall and see what was going on. She was going to raise hell. She was going to be naughty. She was going to be a bad girl. The dinner and the g-string didn't work.

Point of View:

Lucy smiles. "What would you like on your hot dog, sir?"

Another Point of View:

Oh, Lucy . . . I want you on my hot dog . . . Lucy, Lucy, Lucy . . . you and your yellow hair, yellow like those banana shakes you make . . . oh, Lucy.

"Relish," Randy says.

Climax:

Be naughty, be naughty, Janice thinks. But the article never showed me how to be naughty. Janice takes the escalator up to The Drinks & Links thinking all the way up: *BE NAUGHTY.* She finds Randy. He is sitting in a yellow plastic chair, eating a hot dog, staring at the cash register. *Be naughty, I am a bad girl:* this is Janice's mantra. She stands in front of her husband, who has yellow mustard on his lips, and says: "Randy, what the hell is going on? You're a mess, there's mustard everywhere and you're not coming home for dinner anymore. Speak to me!" But Randy is silent, sees right through her body, sees yellow Lucy pouring coffee into a mug.

"Randy, Randy, for Christ's sake, get a grip, look at me!" But Randy keeps looking through her body, keeps seeing Lucy. Another customer, who's sitting three feet away, watches their exchange. He eats a Caesar salad from the deli beside The Drinks & Links, while occasionally smiling at Janice, for support it seems. A navy suitcase is about two feet away from the man's feet, but it's obviously his. *Be naughty, be naughty.* As smoothly as Lucy gives back change, the man's navy suitcase is in Janice's right hand. And she is out the door.

Epiphany:

Janice runs through the parking lot, unaware that the owner of the suitcase is about twenty feet behind her and Randy is about twenty feet behind him. Randy is out of breath and so he watches Janice rifle through the navy suitcase. Even at a fair distance, he can see that she is smiling and laughing and hugging that stranger. The sky is very blue, it tints her face a light blue, her eyes are sparkling (they are almost the same colour as her sweater). And then he sees Janice and all the blueness of her.

Another Epiphany:

Janice runs through the parking lot, slowing down as she approaches the Chevron gas station. "Hey, can I get the key to your bathroom. I also need to change a tire—how about a crowbar while you're at it?"

Once she locks herself alone in the cubicle, she forces the suitcase open: Clothes. Men's Clothes. Toiletries. Irish Spring Soap. Crest Toothpaste. Shampoo. He is very clean, she thinks. Clothes. 36 waist, 34 leg—much smaller than Randy. Just clothes. She smiles when she hears the sirens and shouts in the direction of the paper towel dispenser, *I AM A BAD GIRL!*

The heat made them deaf.

She was told not to look.

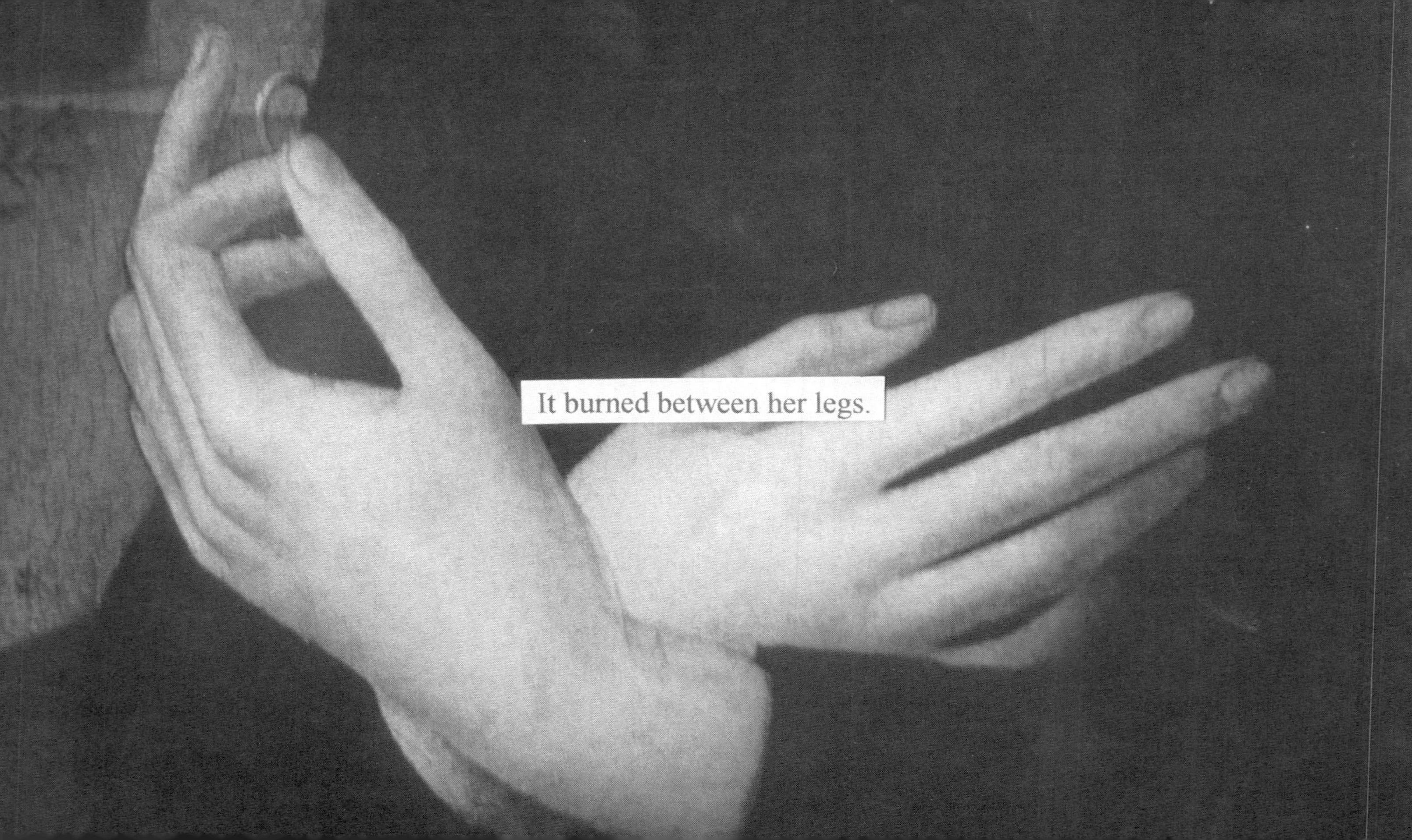
It burned between her legs.

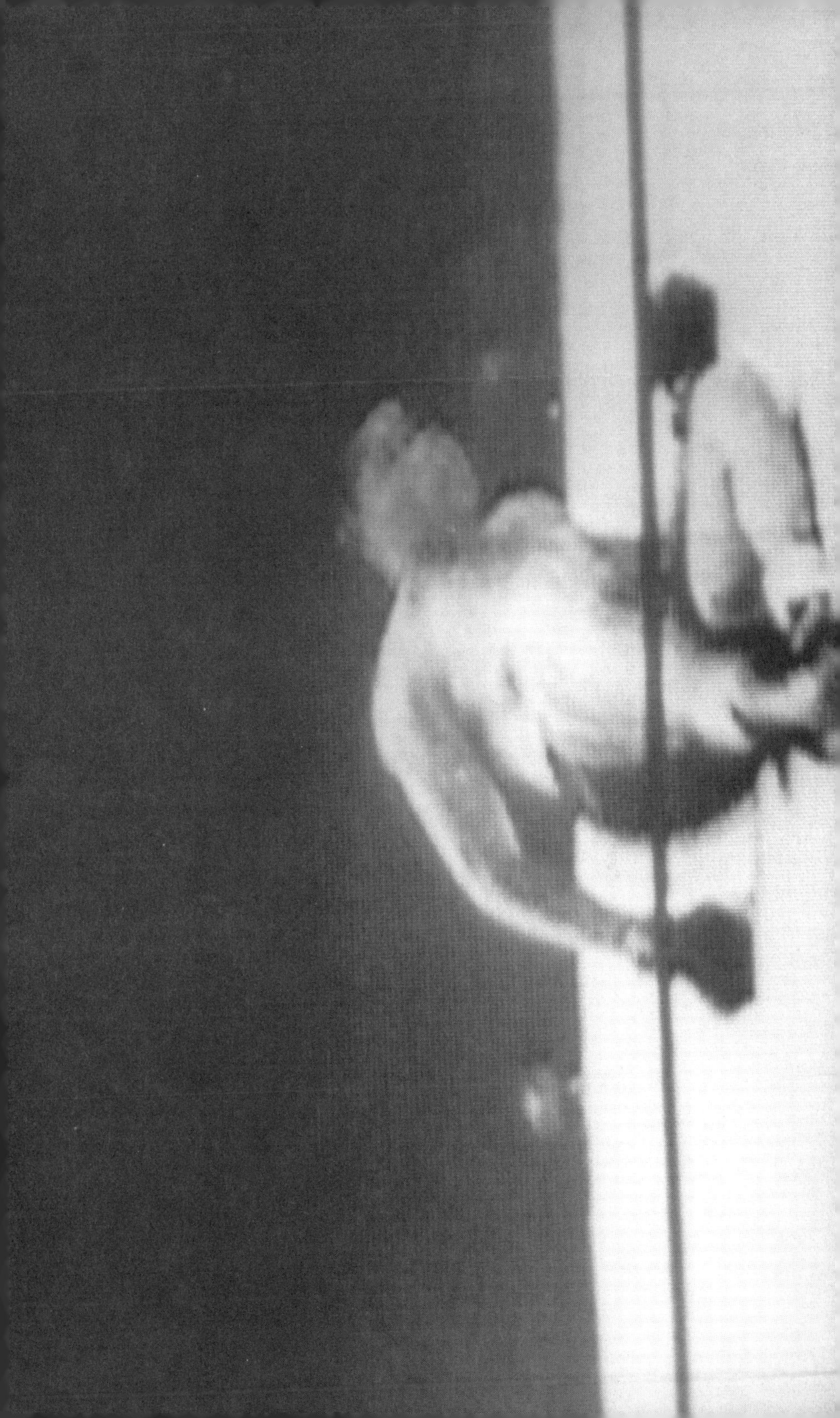

STEVEN SHAVIRO

abducted

ABDUCTED. The stories are everywhere: in books and films, on talk shows, on the World Wide Web. Dr. John E. Mack of Harvard estimates that as many as several million Americans may have been abducted by aliens in UFOs. His 1994 book *Abduction: Human Encounters With Aliens* presents representative case histories. Budd Hopkins gives a more detailed report of one case in his 1987 book *Intruders*, later a TV miniseries. And Whitley Strieber provides a gripping first-person account of being abducted in his 1987 book *Communion*, later turned into a film. All the stories are quite similar. The aliens are gray, hairless, about four feet tall, with leathery skin and vaguely humanoid features. Their eyes are deep, black, and unblinking, and have hypnotic power. If you look directly into them, yours will crumble and you are paralyzed. The encounters usually take place at night. The victims are mostly white Middle Americans. They are snatched from their beds or their cars, and taken aboard a UFO. They are stretched out on a sort of operating table. First, the aliens take tissue samples. They impress strange marks on the skin, like stigmata. They insert small implants into the abductee's body. They stick long needles through the eyes, nose, or ears, and on into the brain. Then they bring out the notorious anal probe. Many witnesses have described this device. It's a thick metal rod, about fourteen inches long. At one end, there is a tiny sphere like a ball bearing. The sphere is surrounded by little prongs that enclose it as in a wire cage, or open outward to let it roam freely. When Strieber was penetrated by this tool, he says, "it seemed to swarm into me as if it had a life of its own . . . I had the impression that I was being raped . . . I have never felt so tiny, so helpless." No part of the body is safe from these intrusions. But all in all, the aliens are less interested in our anuses and brains than in our genitalia. They attach suction devices to men's penises, milking them for sperm. They implant embryos in women's wombs, only to extract them again a few months later. The little alien fetuses are then placed in transparent tanks. One abductee saw rows of these tanks stacked up against the wall, like a display of Barbie dolls in a toy store window. Perhaps the aliens are trying to breed a hybrid species, mixing their genes with ours. Or maybe they can't even reproduce on their own, but need help from our bodies and DNA. We service them as bees do flowers. In any case, the aliens seem clinically detached during these procedures. Sex is evidently not joyous or fulfilling for them. "They don't know what a porn movie is," one victim remarks. "[They don't] understand the concept of voyeurism or anything like that." Their interest in us is not prurient, nor do they bear us malice. It's just that they don't realize how much it all hurts. As Hopkins puts it, "they simply appear unable for the most part to understand us, our feelings, our terror, our love for one another." They fail to grasp even the simplest things about us, like how we dress or how we do our hair. Human emotions are "like candy" or "like a drug" to them, one abductee explains, a dangerous luxury in which they dare not indulge. No wonder our close encounters end in mutual misunderstanding. Maybe their hybrid breeding project is an effort to close the gap. If so, it is an endeavor gone sadly awry. They re-abduct women whose wombs they have previously 'borrowed.' The surrogate mother is brought to meet her putative offspring. The aliens seem to expect some grand scene of reconciliation. But it's hard for us to regard these young with ordinary human affection. They do not seem like anything of ours. They are silent, frail, and disturbingly listless. They show no signs of love, nor even of recognition. They require a colder, more rarefied atmosphere than we can provide. No, these odd children do not join the human to the alien. Rather, they are living reminders of how vast a distance remains. They embody, not our hopes and dreams, but something we cannot even imagine. If they are a part of us, it's the part that we have lost and will never find again. The yearning we feel towards them is like an ache in a phantom limb. What does it mean to be intimate, against your will, with a stranger? Once you have been abducted, you are stranded between two worlds. You've been exiled from the one, without finding refuge in the other.

blood

BLOOD. "In bed under Caddie touching me, our lips parted, spitting blood. I began happening out of nowhere. This was the beginning of bleeding. Straight into Caddie. You will not die from bleeding. I am not among the dead. My sister's breath strange and unsettling. You will bleed into life, not into death. Caddie exhausting her body into me. And between my thighs I felt the making of language." This is Doug Rice, in his 1996 novel *Blood of Mugwump*. The book might be called a romance about three generations of transsexual vampires. But that makes it seem more linear than it actually is. Nothing in this novel is quite solid. Everything oozes and runs, in a viscous flow. The book is filled with mud, blood, and saliva. These are dense, gooey substances, thicker than water. They congeal, time and again, into flesh and into language. But they never maintain any one shape for very long. They are always bleeding into new configurations. The novel is a flux of words, meeting a flux of bodies. Rice's gorgeous prose stutters and sings by turns. Words cascade in syncopated rhythms. Pronouns shift in gender, person, and number. Sentences break into fragments. Phrases proliferate in kaleidoscopic patterns.

Echoes of other texts (by Faulkner, Joyce, Eliot, and Burroughs) resound from page to page. Utterances arise deep in the body: in the throat, the belly, the cunt. Language is intensely carnal. This gets in the way of meaning. As Doug says of Caddie, "she had always had trouble with sentences, running sense over the tops of things . . . Scattering frozen syllables, lost, on the floor, words were arrested, made to suffer on her tongue." The word becomes flesh, and suffers a kind of Passion. Cosmic confusion ensues. There's no way to distinguish between the genders. Men have cunts, and women have cocks. Bodies are as unstable as words. You can't even tell where one ends and the other begins. Doug and Caddie twist in an eternal dance. She is his sister. But she is also his father. Or else she is his drag persona. Or else he is hers. She is so close, as to suffocate him with her presence. Yet she always manages to evade his touch and his glance. No wonder Doug has no sense of himself. Caddie fucks him senseless. She turns him into a woman, and back into a man. There is no end to these transformations. The novel is full of tales of gender confusion. Doug as a child is seduced by the older girl next door. Doug as an adult is arrested for dressing as a woman. Poppy Torgov, Doug's grandfather, appears as a bearded lady at the County Fair. Grandma Mugwump, Doug's grandmother, is born male. She becomes a woman by devouring female flesh. She recalls when Poppy Torgov told her "how I could become a woman and my cock getting hard just thinking about it." These delirious stories never add up to a plot that you can follow. The book is like a labyrinth with no exits. Time flows backward. Events precede their causes. Caddie talks and talks, "breeding her own ancestors out of the river stories" that she tells. The past is not recovered by this method. Rather, even the present moment turns into a story. It becomes distant and unreal, already drowned in the past. It seems to Doug "as if the past had taken Caddie over the edge into some sort of abyss." But Grandma Mugwump is that abyss, in person. Her monstrous figure is the focus of every story. She spends the entire novel lying sick in bed, endlessly speaking, endlessly dying. Doug and Caddie explore her reeking flesh. They crawl in "the craters on her belly." They unravel the dizzying folds of her cunt. They watch her eyes glow in the dark while she sleeps. They lose themselves in the vast recesses of her bed, and need help to find their way out again. Through all this, Doug learns what it means to be a girl. A cunt is barely visible from the outside. But it contains volumes, and it can swallow up the world. “What do you see?” is the urgent question that Caddie keeps asking Doug. “Tell me what you see.” All he can answer at first is “nothing there.” For you can’t just look at a cunt. You have to touch it and feel it. You have to discover it in your own body. The pain of bleeding finally teaches Doug that yes, something is there. It’s all a matter, Caddie explains to him, of “the control of blood.” Menstruation is the origin of language. Words and blood alike gush from between the thighs. And that is why Doug “will bleed into life, not into death.” He’s bound to this flesh, whether he likes it or not.

from survivor
CHUCK PALAHNIUK

Part of my job is to preview the menu for a dinner party tonight. This means taking a bus from the house where I work to another big house, and asking some strange cook what they expect everybody to eat. Who I work for doesn't like surprises, so part of my job is telling my employers ahead of time if tonight they'll be asked to eat something difficult like a lobster or an artichoke. If there's anything threatening on the menu, I have to teach them how to eat right.

This is what I do for a living.

The house where I clean, the man and the woman who live here are never around. That's just the kind of jobs they have. The only details I know about them are from cleaning what they own. All I can figure out is from picking up after them. Cleaning up the little messes, day after day. Rewinding their videotapes:

Full Service Anal Escorts

The giant breasts of Letha Weapons. The adventures of little Sinderella.

By the time my bus drops me off here, the people who I work for are gone to work downtown. By the time they drive home, I'm back downtown in my housing voucher studio apartment that used to be just a tiny hotel room until somebody crowded in a stove and a fridge to raise the rent. The bathroom's still out in the hall. The only way I ever talk to my employers is by speakerphone. This is just a plastic box sitting on their kitchen counter and yelling at me to get more done. Ezekiel, Chapter Nineteen, Verse Seven:

"And he knew their desolate palaces. . ." something, something, something. You can't keep the whole Bible balanced in your head. You wouldn't have room to remember your name.

The house I've been cleaning the last six years is about what you'd expect, big, and it's in a real tony part of town. This is compared to where I live. All the studio apartments in my neighborhood are the same as a warm toilet seat. Somebody was there just a second before you and somebody will be there the minute you get up.

The part of town where I go to work every morning, there are paintings on the walls. Behind the front door, there are rooms and rooms nobody ever goes into. Kitchens where nobody cooks. Bathrooms that never get dirty. The money they leave out to test me, will I take it, the money is never less than a fifty-dollar bill, dropped behind the dresser as if by accident. The clothes they own look designed by an architect.

Next to the speakerphone is a fat daily planner book they keep full of things for me to get done. They want me to account for my next ten years, task by task. Their way, everything in your life turns into an item on a list. Something to accomplish. You get to see how your life looks flattened out.

The shortest distance between two points is a time line, a schedule, a map of your time, the itinerary for the rest of your life.

Nothing shows you the straight line from here to death like a list.

"I want to be able to look at your planner," the speakerphone yells at me, "and know exactly where I can find you at four o'clock on this day five years from now. I want you to be that exact."

Seeing it down in black and white, somehow you're always disappointed in your life expectancy. How little you'll really get done. The resumé of your future.

It's two o'clock Saturday afternoon so according to my daily planner, I'm about to boil five lobsters for them to practice eating. That's how much money they make.

The only way I can afford to eat veal is when I smuggle it home on the bus sitting in my lap.

The secret to boiling a lobster is simple. First you fill a kettle with cold water and a pinch of salt. You can use equal parts of water and vermouth or vodka. You can add some seaweed to the water for a stronger flavor. These are the basics they teach in Home Economics.

Most everything else I know is from the messes these people leave behind.

Just ask me how to get bloodstains out of a fur coat.

No, really, go ahead.

Ask me.

The secret is cornmeal and brushing the fur the wrong way. The tricky part is keeping your mouth shut.

To get blood off of piano keys, polish them with talcum powder or powdered milk.

This isn't the most marketable job skill, but to get bloodstains out of wallpaper, put on a paste of cornstarch and cold water. This will work just as well to get blood out of a mattress or a davenport. The trick is to forget how fast these things can happen. Suicides. Accidents. Crimes of passion.

Just concentrate on the stain until your memory is completely erased. Practice really does make perfect. If you could call it that.

Ignore how it feels when the only real talent you have is for hiding the truth. You have a God-given knack for committing a terrible sin. It's your calling. You have a natural gift for denial. A blessing.

If you could call it that.

Even after sixteen years of cleaning people's houses, I want to think the world is getting better and better, but really I know it's not. You want there to be some improvement in people, but there won't be. And you want to think there's something you can get done.

Cleaning this same house every day, all that gets better is my skill at denying what's wrong.

God forbid I should ever meet who I work for in person.

Please don't get the idea I don't like my employers. The caseworker has gotten me lots worse postings. I don't hate them. I don't love them, but I don't hate them. I've worked for lots worse.

Just ask me how to get urine stains out of drapes and a tablecloth.

Ask me what's the fastest way to hid bullet holes in a living room wall. The answer is toothpaste. For larger calibers, mix a paste of equal parts starch and salt.

Call me the voice of experience.

Five lobsters is how many I figure they'll take to learn the tricky details of getting the back open. The carapace, I figure. Inside's the brain or the heart you're supposed to be hunting for. The trick is to put the lobsters in the water and then turn up the heat. The secret is to go slow. Allow at least thirty minutes for the water to reach a hundred degrees. This way, the lobsters are supposed to die a painless death.

My daily planner tells me to keep busy, polishing the copper the best way, with half a lemon dipped in salt.

These lobsters we have to practice with are called Jumbos since they're around three pounds apiece. Lobsters under a pound are called Chickens. Lobsters missing a claw are called Culls. The ones I take out of the refrigerator packed in wet seaweed will need to boil about half an hour. This is more stuff you learn in Home Economics.

Of the two large forward claws, the larger claw lined with what look like molars is called the Crusher. The smaller claw lined with incisors is called the Cutter. The smaller side legs are called the Walking Legs. On the underside of the tail are five rows of small fins called Swimmerets. More Home Economics. If the front row of swimmerets is soft and feathery, the lobster is female. If the front row is hard and rough, the lobster is male.

If the lobster is female, look for a bony heart-shaped hollow between the two rear walking legs. This is where the female will still be carrying live sperm if she's had sex within the past two years.

The speakerphone rings while I'm setting the lobsters, three male and two female, no sperm, in the pot on the stove.

The speakerphone rings as I turn up the heat just another notch.

The speakerphone rings while I wash my hands.

The speakerphone rings while I go pour myself a cup of coffee and mix in cream and sugar.

The speakerphone rings while I take a handful of seaweed from the lobster bag and sprinkle it on top of the lobsters in the pot. One lobster lifts a crusher claw for a stay of execution. Crusher claws and cutter claws, they're all rubber-banded.

The speakerphone rings while I go wash and dry my hands again.

The speakerphone rings, and I answer it.

Gaston House, I say.

"Gaston *Residence!*" the speakerphone yells at me. "Say it, Gaston *Residence!* Say it the way we told you how!"

What they teach you in Home Economics is it's correct to call a house a *residence* only in printing and engraving. We've gone over this a million times.

I drink a little coffee and fiddle with the heat under the lobsters. The speakerphone keeps yelling, "Is anyone there? Hello? Have we been cut off?"

This couple I work for, at one party they were the only guests who didn't know to lift the doily with the finger bowl. Since then, they've been addicted to learning etiquette. They still say it's pointless, it's useless, but they're terrified of not knowing every little ritual.

The speakerphone keeps yelling, "Answer me! Damn it! Tell me about the party tonight! What kind of food are we going up against? We've been worried sick all day!"

I look in the cabinet over the stove for the lobster gear, the nut-crackers and nutpicks and bibs.

Thanks to my lessons, these people know all three acceptable ways to place your dessert silver. It's my doing that they can drink iced tea the right way with the long spoon still in the glass. This is tricky, but you have to hold the spoon handle between your index and middle fingers, against the edge of the glass opposite your mouth. Be careful to not poke your eye out. Not a lot of people know this way. You see people taking the wet spoon out and looking for a place to set it and not wreck the tablecloth. Or worse, they just put it anywhere and leave a wet tea stain.

When the speakerphone goes silent, then and only then do I start.

I ask the speakerphone, Are you listening?

I tell the speakerphone, Picture a dinner plate.

Tonight, I say, the spinach soufflé will be at the one-o'clock position. The beets thing will be at four o'clock. A meat thing with slivered almonds was going to be on the other half of the plate in the nine-o'clock position. To eat it, the guests would have to use a knife. And there are going to be bones in the meat.

This is the best posting I've ever had, no kids, no cats, no-wax floors, so I don't want to botch it. If I didn't care, I'd start telling who I work for to do any monkey business I could imagine. Like: You eat the sorbet by licking it out of the bowl, dog-dish fashion.

Or: Pick up the lamb chop with your teeth and shake your head vigorously, side to side.

And what's terrible is they'd probably do this. It's because I've never steered them wrong, they trust me.

Except for teaching them etiquette, my toughest challenge is living down to their expectations.

Ask me how to repair stab holes in nightgowns, tuxedos, and hats. My secret is a little clear nail polish on the inside of the puncture.

Nobody teaches you all the job skills you need in Home Economics, but over enough time, you pick them up. In the church district where I grew up, they teach you the way to make candles dripless is to soak them in strong salt water. Store candles in the freezer until ready to use. That's their kind of household hint. Light candles with a strand of raw spaghetti. Sixteen years I've been cleaning for people in their homes, and never has anybody asked me to walk around with a piece of spaghetti on fire in my hand.

No matter what they stress in Home Economics, it's just not a priority in the outside world.

For example, no one teaches you that green-tinted moisturizer will help hide red, slapped skin. And any gentleman who's ever been backhanded by a lady with her diamond ring should know a styptic pencil will stop the bleeding. Close the gash with a dab of Super Glue and you can be photographed at a movie premier, smiling and without stitches or a scar.

Always keep a red washcloth around for wiping up blood, and you'll never have a stain to presoak.

My daily planner tells me I'm sharpening a butcher knife.

About the dinner tonight, I keep briefing who I work for about what to expect.

The important part is not to panic. Yes, there's going to be a lobster they'll have to deal with.

There's going to be a single saltcellar. A game course will be served after the roast. The game is going to be squab. It's a kind of bird, and if there's anything more complicated to eat than a lobster, it's a squab. All those little bones you have to dismantle, everybody dressed up for their dissection. Another wine will come after the aperitif, the sherry with the soup course, the white wine with the lobster, the red with the roast, another red wine with the greasy ordeal of the squab. By this time, the table will be spotted with everybody's piddling island archipelagoes of dressings and sauces and wine sprayed across the white tablecloth.

This is how my job goes. Even in a good posting, nobody wants to know where the male guest of honor is supposed to sit.

That exquisite dinner your teachers in Home Economics talked about, the pause with fresh flowers and demitasse after a perfect day of poise and elegant living, well, nobody gives a rat's ass about that.

Tonight, at some moment between the soup course and the roast, everybody at the table will get to mutilate a big dead lobster. Thirty-four captains of industry, thirty-four successful monsters, thirty-four acclaimed savages in black tie will pretend they know how to eat.

And after the lobster, the footmen will present hot finger bowls with floating slices of lemon, and these thirty-four botched autopsies will end with garlic and butter up to the elbow of every sleeve and every smiling greasy face will look up from sucking out meat from some cavity in the thorax.

After seventeen years of working in private houses every day, the things I know the most about are slapped faces, creamed corn, black eyes, wrenched shoulders, beaten eggs, kicked shins, scratched corneas, chopped onions, bites of all sorts, nicotine stains, sexual lubricants, knocked-out teeth, split lips, whipped cream, twisted arms, vaginal tears, deviled ham, cigarette burns, crushed pineapple, hernias, terminated pregnancies, pet stains, shredded coconut, gouged eyes, sprains, and stretch marks.

The ladies who you work for, after they sob for hours on end, make them use blue or mauve eyeliner to make their bloodshot eyes look whiter. The next time someone socks a tooth out of her husband's mouth, save the tooth in a glass of milk until he can see the dentist. In the meantime, mix zinc oxide and oil of cloves into a white paste. Rinse the empty socket and pack it with the paste for a quick and easy filling that hardens lickety-split.

For tear stains in a pillow case, treat them the same way you would a perspiration stain. Dissolve five aspirin in water and daub the stain until it's gone. Even if there's a mascara stain, the problem's solved.

If you could call it solved.

Whether you clean a stain, a fish, a house, you want to think you're making the world a better place, but really you're just letting things get worse. You think maybe if you just work harder and faster, you can hold off the chaos, but then one day you're changing a patio light bulb with a five-year life span and you realize how you'll only be changing this light maybe ten more times before you'll be dead.

Time is running out. There isn't the kind of energy you used to have. You start to slow down.

You start to give in.

This year there's hair on my back, and my nose keeps getting bigger. How my face looks every morning is more and more what you'd call a mug.

After working in these rich houses, I know the best way to get blood out of the trunk of a car is not to ask any questions.

The speakerphone is saying, "Hello?"

The best way to keep a good job is just do what they want.

The speakerphone is saying, "Hello?"

To get lipstick out of a collar, rub in a little white vinegar.

For stubborn protein-based stains, like semen, try rinsing with cold salt water, then wash as usual.

This is valuable on-the-job training. Feel free to take notes.

To pick up broken glass from that jimmied bedroom window or smashed highball, you can blot up even the tiniest shards with a slice of bread.

Stop me if you already know all this.

The speakerphone is saying, "Hello?"

Been there. Done that.

What else they teach you in Home Economics is the correct way to respond to a wedding invitation. How to address the Pope. The right way to monogram silver. In the Creedish church school, they teach how the world can be a perfect elegant little stage play of perfect manners where you're the director. The teachers, they paint a picture of dinner parties where everyone will already know how to eat a lobster.

Then it's not.

Then all you can do is get lost in the tiny details of every day doing the same tasks over and over.

There's a fireplace to clean.

There's a lawn to mow.

Turn all the bottles in the wine cellar.

There's the lawn to mow, again.

There's the silver to polish.

Repeat.

Still, just one time, I'd like to prove I know something better. I can do more than just cover up. The world can be a lot better than we settle for. All you have to do is ask.

No, really, go ahead. Ask me.

How do you eat an artichoke?

How do you eat asparagus?

Ask me.

How do you eat a lobster?

The lobsters in the pot look dead enough so I lift one out. I tell the speakerphone, First, twist off each of the big front claws.

The other lobsters I'll put in the refrigerator for them to practice taking apart. To the speakerphone I say, Take notes.

I crack the claws and eat the meat inside.

Then I bend the lobster backward until its tail snaps away from its body. Snap off the tip of the tail, the Telson, and use a seafood fork to push out the tail meat. Remove the intestinal vein that runs the length of the tail. If the vein is clear, the lobster hasn't eaten anything for a while. A thick dark vein is fresh and still full of dung.

I eat the tail meat.

The seafood fork, I tell the speakerphone with my mouth full, the seafood fork is the little baby fork with three prongs.

Next, you unhinge the back shell, the carapace, from the body, and eat the green digestive gland called the Tomalley. Eat the copper-based blood that congeals into white gunk. Eat the coral-colored immature egg masses.

I eat them all.

Lobsters have what you'd call an "open" circulatory system where the blood just sloshes around inside their cavities, bathing the different organs.

The lungs are spongy and tough, but you can eat them, I tell the speakerphone and lick my fingers. The stomach is the tough sac of what look like teeth just behind the head. Don't eat the stomach.

I dig around inside the body. I suck the little meat out of each walking leg. I bite off the tiny gill bailers. I bypass the ganglia of the brain.

I stop.

What I find is impossible.

The speakerphone is yelling, "Okay, now what? Was that everything? What's there left to eat?"

This can't be happening because according to my daily planner, it's almost three o'clock. I'm supposed to be outside digging up the garden. At four, I'll rearrange the flower beds. At five-thirty, I'll pull up the salvia and replace them with Dutch iris, roses, snapdragons, ferns, ground clover.

The speakerphone is yelling, "What is happening there? Answer me! What's gone wrong?"

I check my schedule, and it says I'm happy. I'm productive. I work hard. It's all right down here in black and white. I'm getting things done.

The speakerphone yells, "What do we do next?"

Today is just one of those days the sun comes out to really humiliate you.

The speakerphone yells, "What's there left to do?"

I ignore the speakerphone because there's nothing left to do. Almost nothing's left.

And maybe this is just a trick of light, but I've eaten almost the whole lobster before I notice the heart beat.

From above gravity seemed to arrest the stars.

On the ground heaven as close as a breath of smoke.

seeping

DAVID PINSON

Men said minnows, said minnowy.

Not quite fish, we lay below like fish.

So named, less one more of us to measure, extraction is what we meant to survive.

Men offered other colors for our skin. One gave matches a lick—the lit end! One bragged to dragging home bacon. One ate bacon, leaving us not any nor some. We were made to take bacon, to then seep to our shore below where we raised no peep and slept like cats asleep with ears receiving each other's little motions and those from those bigger of us above.

Stomping, would come in men. Man after man. Men over us. Serving men, we learned leanless cuts of meat, veggers, saucepans, oven mittens and plastic not porcelain plates, tables four- sometimes three-legged, ashy beer bottles broken, and utensils washed each and every way, mostly by us, us of us seeking to seep beneath.

Sometimes seeping was breathing.

Stories we sought not to say. About men. About the small one, Brinnie. About the animal. About a space not a basement but a place under joisting.

About men, again. Man after man. Men after minnows.

We may say this now. It is old water, as old as water as winter water is old, saying this is, we mean. Saying this here are adults, which are us, which is us older than us before, still us minus men and the one of us the little one, and certainly sans the measurings measured on the wall.

The biggest came at us a blamer. And you! And you! All of you! All of you to him would be all of us to us, the seepers. No nails grew on his fingers across our cheeks; we were made to chew them. The stubble of his club chin numbed our skins.

We had reason to lean.

We ate milk solidified from the fridge.

The bacon-bringer shouted. He screamed about our spines making straighter the measuring wall look. His breath air came out fecal, copper, some clay. Ladders of pencilings laddered the wall alongside the stairway. Brinnie's measurings stopped we were not— still are not— sure when.

When?

The bringer of bacon would whisper. He'd say, "Minnowsminnowsminnowsminnowsminnowsminnows."

Clots in our gills, beneath the surface of two-by-sixes, next to the furnace, near the pipes that were water and gas, this is where we coiled for radon to come, for Brinnie, for extraction.

BrinnieBrinnieBrinnieBrinnie!

Then, her name unspoken.

The animal came one morning running, grousing. Men decided a bowl a day from a bag kept ready, and water in a big butter tub licked clean by the animal's black lapper. The animal had hair of ferment; Brinnie's was maybe woven with the sun.

In the crawl space there was the fact of boards, an effort of cardboard shoring, the issue of string-pulling for light. There was the bedding of newsprint bedding. There was the door not a door through to the outside we could not go.

Ponded.

The men said ponded.

child poems

BRIGID YUKMAN

#1

I dreamt last night that I was taking care of a child, like I used to take care of my sister. Only the house had so many doors and a strong wind was blowing. I kept losing her. She would go into another room, and I was afraid she'd go outside and be lost. And my heart flew ahead of my voice calling, calling. There were so many doors and windows. The wind raced through them. Then I'd see her little head, but she'd disappear again. And I kept thinking next time I won't find her, she'll be gone. I looked and looked and for a long time couldn't find her, but then I turned a corner and there she was. And very slowly, so as not to frighten her, I sat down by her and I took her into my arms and held her and she laughed. And I said, little one, I'm going to teach you a song to remember. When I sing: Little cup, little cup, you sing back to me, I'm the cup, I'm the cup. So we sat singing to ourselves. And then we did it backwards and she sang little cup and I sang I'm the cup. I prayed that she would remember and that she would sing out to me and back to me wherever she was so that I would be able to find her. So that I could let her go through the door.

Cup

Cat sleeps in my lap,

A child's sleeping head over my heart like a dark
Pulls her seaward, to the iris, a lost mother opening her womb.
Asleep she remembers

And forgives me.
I make my beating pulse a bird
To take her home. She rides head listening

At my heart in search of paradise.

I believe her, hold her, go with her,
Stay alive, let my strangeness become
Her refrain, let it carry her far as she will go:

Sleep little cat, in your going you are
the cup of life, the cup, the cup.

And in thc corner, waiting, a dancer's sparkling eye,

(Do you dance?)

Loving eye. Fear, the dancer, daring, flourishing the filled cup.

#2

My younger sister thinks I need to see a birth. She dreamt that I was at her birth, and everyone moved to make a space for me to come forward, and look.

Once, after a massage, a woman asked me, is there anything your body wants to do? But I didn't know. Then she said, you can give birth to yourself if you want.

You see, we don't have to. There are a lot of reasons not to be born. Good reasons. Movement over water Voices weaving the night sky. Animal laughter. Stillness. A stone's heft inside the earth. The brush of bird wing like a soft cheek. Golden fish swimming freely into the deep beds where a body's heart and sex will be.

#3

Riddle

The field waits to be hunted
but the house is warm.

If only the door would stay open.

There may be small animals in the walls.
Buttons of light move when she walks.
Paper beds to keep warm.

Listen like sleep.

I knead her breasts for milk she does not have.

#4

Why would we want to be born into a body?
Why look up at the stars?

Imagine a room without doors.

Or being born into the body of a bird, small, quick,
gliding

(O happy fall)

But I did want it. I wanted to push myself away from myself. I wanted the pulse of blood. The fiber of my own muscle. To body forth. The rise of sex amazed, up from the root. I wanted memory. So I pushed and pushed. I pushed into a white room

a sky turned on its side, wide.

I slipped behind a white wall

Enfold me, wing.

I pushed myself out of my body and held myself and sucked at the salt of my tears and my skin.

"We don't even know we're born"

#5

Doors

A room full of people.
A room with closed doors.
Someone opens the doors,
someone else closes them

like
heart valves.

A wind.

Small white stones on the beach.
A pattern of flowers on the wall, a flock of birds across the window.

Everything over us needs children
to unfold itself.

madonna

The sky,

come to the window

passing over the heart
is blue.

Woman held like a child.

Woman looking up,
out
through
at
the sky.

An arm rests across her upper frame.

Woman looking at the sky
—no, seeing the sky.

Her eyes are blue
of themselves,
and of what she sees.

In the corner
of one eye,

sitting next to the sky
look—
a small mother
leaning over her tiny child.

#6

O something to catch her fall—

Someone, holding something in her hands,
remembers herself as a child and the smell of her mother's hair and
decides to love.

O something to catch her fall—
to land as birds do, however

gone over to flight and the intercourse with air,

> *(quick drowning, rush of space through the lungs,*
> *as if a loose string pulls taut*
> *like the pitch of a plucked horsehair)*

to go to ground.

A front porch,
jutting crag,
flowering, flowering branch,

sill wide enough,
near, down, at the tit, love.

#7

And the heart has already gone out into the woods alone
before the school child prepares for the first day of school,
with his new pencils and notebook and lunch in a bag,
before the mother sends her boy, she sends her life
out ahead. He is already in love with the world.
She is already carrying stones in her pocket
to keep her feet on the ground.
He learns to write his name.
She sings to herself.

#8
night:

So carefully the trees
lay down the night.

The dark is filled with voices.

The phone rings. She lifts
the receiver, heavy with voices,

holds it to her ear,
adjusts her breathing,

The dark is filled

until it is the same rhythm,
then lays the small thing down

like a mother tucking in her child
like a lover letting go of her lover's hand

The dark is filled with children.

And she goes into the dark.

#9
day:

Newborn
so old,
she is lacking
the middle of her life,
wanting the bridge,
the circling out
from a center,
the turn in the middle
of the floor.

She is willing
to pull the sky down.
To choose again,
with heart,
with violence,

to let go of everything
like a bride
for the want of something unknown

to arrange a house

or burn it down,

keep a fire

cross a shelf,
a barrier reef. . .

#10

In the great night my heart will go out
Toward me the darkness comes rattling
In the great night my heart will go out
(Papago Indian)

the story of my mother's death: with a recitation by queen shaharazad

DIANA ABU-JABER

My mother's hand lowers, touches her hair, pulls the loose strands back. She loses sight of the jeep taking me away to America. Her face is startling, luminous; it gives the onlooker the sense of a bird whisked from darkness to light.

Her eyes are a story that should not have been written; to see her face is to look through a private letter. People turn away as she approaches, fingers tremble, drop the letter. There are things that are too hard to read. There are things that demand to be read; the page at the bottom of the desk calls its secret song.

So she turns back the flap of our tent. Her mouth tastes like tears, eyes swollen, lulled by grief: she is swimming in the dark, sleepy air. There is a sunburst of pain in the center of her head, there is a hand prying apart her ribs like opening a book. There are tracks in her brown skin where the tears should be. There is a golden apple by her hand, heart-fat, full of poison.

When she eats it, she knows she will have just enough time to lick almost all the traces away, to pack what remains in the trunk, to push the trunk into the road, addressed and sealed, where someone will find it, where someone will know what to do. No time for a farewell note.

I want to forget what I've read in her face; I want to look away from it already. I'd like to drink some drug of my own, look into the sun and not feel it, not care at all. How delicate love is, how ephemeral, how time eases everything, blessed relief, grinding every face, laugh, sweetness, cruelty, to dust, to dried herb, to cinnamon and turmeric. Nothing left but fine powder and the wind, sweet wind carries every trace away, borne inside its unknowable body. Even as I devour your body I forget you, even as I stare at your face I feel nothing; love cannot survive.

Mother, taste the sweet dreams, the cherry bark, bitter nut and root and breath of dirt, deep earth. The demon comes up, called from beneath the bottom of the earth, salt of the sea. Press your tongue to sweet forgetfulness, banishment of woes. The ifrit rises, Queen Shaharazad appears to you from between the dunes and begins to tell the story of Alf Laila Wa Laila, night of nights, a thousand nights and one, evening of primrose scenting the air, birds like sweet bees rising. The walls of the tent move closer to listen. Close your eyes—the storyteller's voice is sweet—turn your eyes away from memory: daughter, husband, homeland.

The Queen comes, a torch in the shadows, and it is day.
She says: There was and there was not
fat olive trees, endless, ancient orchards.
The figs wove their fingers, bent their backs.
Voices rinsing the air as many as
feathers on the nightingale.

Shaharazad pauses, touches your face. She tosses her runner of hair over one shoulder, neck painted by the moon. She is holding your hand. She is speaking, her words are red bursts, pomegranate seeds, red melon sugar, her tongue a sweet dart:

I will tell the tender tale of Princess Jasmine and Prince Almond.

My mother is too sleepy to listen. Too sleepy to be yemmah, my mother, any longer. Your arms whitening in sleep, losing memory's long ropes, winding sheet of nothingness. No use for your long struggle, long walk; the earth fades from you as camphor melts in the sun.

Prince Almond lived the outer life of a shepherd, but his interior being was occupied with love.

Mother, did you once love, brilliantly, heart open as an autumn rose? Did you ever say, "I love you more than all others. I shall love you forever"? Ever memorize the scent of the lover's skin, the shape of the lover's body, so in sleep you return to its form, lover's name in your dreaming mouth, the absence of the lover like a cleft in the body?

At night, he stayed in the garden with his mistress Jasmine.

Or did you bind your love up in your arms, carry it hitched to your hip, a basket of fruit? Were you stingy with love. Did you parcel it out, little sweet-meats, give it only to the baby in her blanket.

But who may hold even the most hidden happiness to be safe forever from the jealousy of censure?

Were you ever jealous, frightened, shaken to the bones, drowned in light?

"Your wives and daughers are the chief of your foes . . . They lack both reason and probity. They were born of a twisted rib."

Dear rib, little bent bone, bit of skin and spit, dear thing alone on this the darkest of nights, night of nights, scented with the eight scents of passion. This night floats free and alone, like the pulse in a lover's wrist, the sugar of his tongue. This night is the darkest of darks, torn curtain. I listen, waiting for the dark judgement of the story-King.

"Shame of your fathers," the King cried. "Until today our dwelling was free from the thorns and bitter herbs of shame."

Shaharazad and her violet eyes, her black river of hair, she winks at me, your daughter, watching from the distance of memory. There are streams of Persian, Arabic, French, English, Turkish, Hebrew, Latin, German beating at the banks, copper-colored waters. She is waving goodbye. Oh don't leave now, Queen Shaharazad, please finish your story . . .

When he had punished his daughter, King Akbar gave orders for the destruction of her shepherd.

The shepherd guards the moon, silvery-haired fields, the backs of sheep, silver-haired goat, and the ravening pig-deer. Do you see it? The voices, flute, wine-notes, thunder, bawl and complaint. Danger is all around them, vast under the two-horned star.

But the sweet-eyed prince tamed the wild animals with the glory of his playing.

He plays music of revelation, opening, rescue. A world of touch, song like prayer, music as meditation, transfiguration. His music says: do your work, your chores, your study, voice lessons, language lessons. Your words my mouth: say it like this. No, like this. Lips and tongue and mouth like so. Watch me. Let me watch you. Blow on my face, speak from *here,* from the center of the heart. Here.

Jasmine secretly glided from the chamber in her gold robes and fled to Almond.

Aleph, baa, taa, thaa, jeem, haa . . . *lawz,* almond, *ifrit,* spirit, *akbar,* big, *souq,* market.

The storyteller says:

There are few upon this earth worthy of happiness, worthy to take the road which leads to happiness, worthy to draw near the house of happiness.

The poison my mother has swallowed has ticked through her body, combed and parted her blood, the blood of a young woman, younger than I am now. She is sleeping her way into death, no longer my mother, with arms the color of water, neck and hands the color of wheat.

Not quite alive and not quite dead, the woman who used to be my mother lies flat on the prayer rug with the sides of our tent working like a bellows, the wind surging with its breath. Anvil of air. It will only take a few hours for her to die this way.

King Shahriyar's anguish over his first wife's infidelity drove him to exact revenge: to consume a virgin a night, raping her by moonrise and murdering her by daybreak. His domain bowed their heads to this wrath, offering up their women: who can refuse the rage of kings?

King Shahriyar with his broken soul, his heart snapped like a dry bone, his violated dreams, his rubbed-raw days, he brought all this to Shaharazad. He imprisons her, invades her, occupies her night after Arabian night so the nights become one night, so Shaharazad dwells in a single dimension of night; it is the food she eats and the water she drinks.

Shaharazad can smell blood on his skin. She worries that she herself may acquire a taste for blood. When her king bends to bury his face in her neck, he murmurs, at last I am home. He murmurs, you are mine. He murmurs, I shall rename you. It is too late for Shaharazad's husband, King Shahriyar, to ask for his wife's forgiveness. Not after one thousand and one nights of stories, after years of his murderous deeds. He granted her life in exchange for her stories.

But, of course, this is all just a story too—and, as students have been saying to teachers since the beginning—what good are stories? Can we eat them when we're hungry? Can they shade us from the sun?

Shaharazad twists her black current of hair in her hand. It is time for her to go home and see to the children. She kisses the brow of the solitary sleeper in her tent, then rises. Wait! I call after her. *Please*. Just one more moment . . .

She pauses. I smell the rosewater in her hair. I want to ask about justice—

Her black eyes are level with the horizon, straight as daggers.

I want to know

Shall I carry this rage in my throat in my hands in my eyes like a heavy stone? Furnace in my belly, ashes beneath my tongue.

Shaharazad smooths her hand over my hair. "On the day of your mother's dying, the scent of Jasmine flower covered the desert. It began from somewhere under your mother's left ring finger and spread until everyone in the camp was looking up. The men grew intoxicated and swayed under its spell. The children turned giddy and silly, or fell asleep where they stood. The women lifted their arms and turned, twining it around their necks and shoulders. The horses laughed and the sheep smiled and the he-camel called to his she-camel.

It covered the desert skies like a wine skin and the sands turned musky and the oases breathed. In some places the men forgot how to use their guns. In other places the women abandoned their guns under bushes, in bits of scrub. In the very farthest corner of the desert, the scent had to stretch and pale and fade until it was little more than a memory of Jasmine. This memory curled itself under the nose of Emir Lawz, the stillest, sharpest-eyed, straightest-backed of all the Bedu. And who knows if he would have smelled it as, at that moment, he was relieving himself in a lush, tall-banked almond grove. Fortunately, however, Emir Lawz, along with the blackest lashes and the thickest hair, had the greatest moustache known to the desert, and this gave the memory a resting place.

The Emir left the grove and the scent of almond retreated, and suddenly his senses were flooded with Jasmine. He was filled with nostalgia, fragments of desires, wishes, bits of thought—in particular of a strong Palestinian woman he had loved, and of her little daughter who was like a piece of moonlight.

For the memory, then, and this fading whiff of Jasmine, he climbed his horse and said goodbye for now to his mother and father and grandmother and grandfather and all his relatives. They waved peaceably, all of them knowing that a Bedouin never leaves his tribe unless under the command of some love spell. And who was to say, as Sitt Boostan, his grandmother pointed out, that he shouldn't obey this crazy spell. For, after all, wasn't there a little bit of silver starting now in his lush hair, a little gray intermingling with that finest of moustaches?

So when he and his spotted horse were gone, the Huwyatat followed at a respectful distance, to help him out of whatever difficulty he might find himself in. But someone who is drawn by the scent of Jasmine loses all sense of day and night, and it was as if in the twinkling of an eye that Emir Lawz found himself approaching the secret encampment, the place he had refused to visit, year after year, when his tribe stopped there, because he knew there was a woman there with a neck like the date palm's curve and hair with the gloss of fresh figs. And she would not have him because she could not bear to travel.

He paused just a moment and this was not merely a pause but a listening. What was this lilt of a man on horseback waiting to hear? What musical note or lyrical word? Then again, this was not merely listening for a sound but a sense, yes, the signal, the whisper of her breath, for she had always made him think of white Jasmine—not the stars of its buds, not the sweet of its perfume, but the inner soul of all Jasmine trees—stem and scent, green and petal, name and song. It seemed to him that she owned the soul of the miraculous flowers that shook at the edges of white sheets of sand.

He waits at the hidden place between the rocks and the wild trees, and there is nothing to hear. The scent of Jasmine has trickled out of his moustache, and there is nothing else, not a pulse or exhalation in the air.

Then he is on foot and running to her tent as he has dreamed himself running so many times before. There is a large wooden trunk in the middle of the path, but there is no one anywhere outside, the flaps of her tent are soaring and falling as if the wind had decided to play only in this one small space.

He is running; everywhere there is light that winnows him away, slipping its hot palms beneath his robes, drinking him as fast as he runs. As he touches the edge of the tent burning with light, he feels that he has already disappeared. He falls into the cool spill of shadow inside, nearly into the arms of the not-quite alive, not-quite dead woman on her rug.

And, oh, if you have not yet tasted grief, not yet held it like a stone in the throat, broken arrow in the heart, not really touched every part and aspect of it, then listen to me: this was grief. He was losing more than a thousand nights of dreams—though certainly there were other women, other dreams, always—but *this* dream, the one before and beyond all others, the one from the throat and the heart, and from underneath the tongue caged in its fence of teeth, this dream of dreams was abandoning him. She was dying of grief, and, as a famous king once remarked, all creatures cry from the pain of separation.

After she has lost everything else in the world, she is suffering from just one particular loss—the much awaited loss of you. She can barely lift her dreaming eyes to the stranger. She is dying. She has lived most of her life with the knowledge of this separation. Knowing she will never see you again.

Acting according to his nature—that of a refined, intelligent, courageous, kind and noble being, he tried not to cry out or frighten her or spoil a moment of her dying.

He did not try to wake her or steal her back with a kiss, he did not try to rub the glow of heat back into her body. He smelled the fruity poison on her breath and surrendered.

Some of us spread the cards across the table, some throw sticks and coins, some look at the weather and stars, some read the script of coffee grounds and tea leaves, some go without sleep and some sleep endlessly, some write letters, tuck pages into bottles or tear the sheets to pieces, some record their dreams and others walk through their dreams, the dance of light-sleeping, the music of the night-birds and stars, wandering through thickets to the ends of the path, as far as night and dreams will let you, and you stand and listen.

He lies beside her on the rug, tucking his body into hers, his head in the cradle of her armpit, like a child sleeping on his mother's breast, and he begins to speak. He is sleep-talking, mapping for her as perfectly and exactly as a Bedouin can—the great star-finder, star-charter—exactly the territory which she is about to enter. He describes for her the bluish-white moonlit sands in the country of death. He tells her how to read the directions of flames, to look for the white camel, to read its expression, the undulation of its limbs across the violet surfaces, to touch its wooly side and follow it across the cool, cool sands, to walk behind the pyramids, to watch the red star that will unpeel itself like an eye, on this, the other side, death's side of nature.

She listens; he can feel her listening, even as her eyes close, even as her heart stops. He feels her waiting, pressing her ear to the glass of her mortality, even as she has died, she lingers just a moment on the other side of death's mirror, waiting for him to finish speaking.

*

The camp came out to watch as he lifted her body on to the horse. No one tried to stop the black-eyed Bedouin who held her upright in one arm as one would hold a living woman. Only my friend Lutfea ran to the horse, skirted its hooves, and grabbed the palm that had fallen loose from the man's grip. Lutfea kissed the fingers once, whispering, "Goodbye," then ran away.

He rode to the center of the desert, the buried heart of it that only the Bedu know. Again, his tribe followed at a discreet distance, a little farther behind this time; many of them wept for the memory of the woman and recalled her girl who was like a spot of moonlight.

When he buried her, wrapped in his own jellabia, his own gold ring on her finger, the desert bowed its head, all its animals sighed, deep from the belly, and there was no more Jasmine in the air. All you could smell was bits of dirts and grasses, insect parts, pieces of faraway fish, and bits of goat flesh, all the innumerable parts of digestion in the animal world, spicing the air, helping the man to weep and weep until he could stand up again. He went to drink from the oasis at the center of the desert, and then he fell to weeping again. This process of drinking and weeping went on for many days, and now and then he thought of her daughter and worried about what happened to her. Did she have enough to eat and drink? Was she cared for and sheltered?

He knew he would have to ride back to the camp to claim the trunk. He slipped her ring from the chain around his neck, slipped it into the trunk, and brought it to the rug merchant, who mailed it all back to you.

After all, it is written: it is better to pray than to sleep.

the egg

CAITLIN SULLIVAN

The last time I saw you was in Mexico where we made love three times in two days in the four rooms of the casita we had rented for a week. It wasn't you, technically, but I'll explain that later, it doesn't really matter.

We stayed only three days which could be why we made love so often and with so much fury. I knew then that I never wanted to see you again because we were the happiest we'd ever been, we were in Mexico, there were no children with us; there was nothing real except the fishing net that hung on the back porch of the casita. It was real because it stank and was in no way romantic and since it didn't belong to us we couldn't throw it away or hide it in the cupboard or even lay it on the ground as a covering; it just insisted on smelling like old wet fish and decaying salt.

So here we are again, you and me. Last time you were dark, your belly round; this time you are tall and fairhaired—again, it doesn't matter. You're sitting in the same place across the table, your eyes don't meet mine, there are the usual circumstances. And if I look into your eyes they're not yours anyway, not familiar. They're gone.

You *are* a little different, I must admit. You're cocking your head in concentration at my sentences. You don't make me explain my terms much at all. You keep stroking my hair and putting your face up close to mine, right *there*, so it's not so easy this time to avoid you. But maybe that's because this is our first time, this time around, and you're following all the rules before you sweep the salt and pepper shakers from the table.

I know I looked different to you last time, too, and maybe you're alive with the sensation of differences, but it's basically the same and we're across the table or a room or a bed even and our words float in my air here. All is weighty with meaning, the silence and the words. And the first thing to go is a memory of how it was easy.

You stood by the bed one morning at the casita with a piece of driftwood in your hand and I woke soon after, rolling sleepily just in time to miss the downward swing of your left arm as the wood grazed my ear and struck the pillow. The old seaweed and dried salt flew from the blow and through its haze I thought I saw a thousand things take place somewhere behind you or perhaps near your left ear. I thought I saw you cry out, I thought I saw you search for more wood, I thought I saw you reach to grab the pillow, I thought I saw the arm that held the wood burst into flame.

But because we were on vacation I did what came to me first. I laughed. I laughed as if I knew you were finished and I was congratulating you. I invited you to pretend to be finished, too, but I knew you weren't and you knew I knew you weren't which is why you were stuck for awhile by how brave and shrewd I was.

Right then you wanted me to grab and pull you to me, completing the arc you had started. But I didn't, which was probably my only real contribution—I didn't. I got up, instead, took the wood from your hand and tossed it onto the living room rug on my way to the kitchen for coffee. You wandered out onto the deck to think about your next move I suppose. You needn't worry, you didn't look confused or even taken aback—you were already dressed, as you recall, which gave you some advantage over me. You had a cigarette going and looked as if you didn't know or care if there were another person in the room which is your usual demeanor anyway. So I made a half pot of coffee as if I were alone, too, which I would be when we got back from Mexico after all, then began to make an elaborate show about that, being alone. But I got bored with this, which you may have known, I no longer wanted to show you I wasn't going to make coffee for you and I came out to where you were and held you from behind and kissed you. I had my eyes closed because I didn't want to see you; I wanted you to see me and I could tell through my lids that you had a ready expression, but I had abandoned the act just then and was improvising.

I went back into the kitchen again, aware that every move could produce some reaction in you, savoring that. We'd never quite been there before, you hanging onto my every move, and as I found the cream and opened the drawer for a spoon I felt my hands sliding along the surface of everything, luxuriating in the time and the feeling of your eyes on me. You weren't so amateur as to watch me at all, mind you, but I was using your knowledge of me to my advantage, for once, and I did everything as I usually did, but a little slower. If you noticed my lingering you no doubt attributed it to your own scrutiny. After all, you had never waited on me before.

I pulled the egg carton from the refrigerator, selecting one of the brown eggs, holding it in my hand. I knew I could drop the egg to the floor; the day was as long as that moment, a year was mine in that moment. I could show you I didn't care at all about the place you'd rented and drop the egg on the floor, throw it against a wall, place it close to the edge of the counter, taking the time to balance it on the grooves of brown grout that held the tiles in place. So I held it a long time in my hand, knowing you would feel the pause, feel me weigh the possibilities. The truth is, I no longer cared about my options, I was contemplating for the thousandth time something I'd heard once about not being able to crush an egg with one hand. It seemed entirely possible to me.

The down on your cheek was as soft and inordinately long as it ever was, and at the same time your eyes were back to steely gray, I saw a little fear in them and I knew I had to stop us somehow and move on to something else. I also knew we were at some synapse where we would soon leave with one suitcase between us or one of us would decide to trek back to the highway alone for a ride.

It could have gone the other way just as easily I see now. I see now that I escaped with my life, probably, although that seems somewhat extreme.

*

You, or whoever you are this time, are not fond of your legs because you think they're skinny and you like to wear boots. You have two daughters—you have a son, too, or perhaps you have a son and a daughter. We fought this morning about whether to have another child, so you must only have one. You—this time—have one child. We fought this morning so it can't even be you I'm talking about because I left you sometime around the Nepal thing.

You think I was chosen from among a thousand applicants to go there but the truth is I was asked to pick up some drugs and I decided to go because a Nepalese jail sounded interesting, I reasoned, and it would be something to tell you later and would explain why I had to leave you after the party at the restaurant. You think I went there on a grant because that's what I told you. I didn't go to jail, nor did I meet with my connection because I forgot the directions. I only knew that it had been a month since I'd seen you and it was time to come home. By then nobody would be looking for me anymore and I could tell everyone why I went. When I got to Customs I was very nervous and considered telling them the whole thing, until I remembered I wasn't carrying any drugs and had not even remembered to obtain them, and it was then I realized I didn't have to go back home at all because I'd lost some time and wasn't sure how long I'd been gone. I knew that because I remember standing in line at the Customs desk waiting to be searched and then breathing a sigh of relief that they would find nothing. I changed my plans right then, starting with asking the Customs agent how long I'd been in Nepal. The most exciting thing was that he answered without judgment, informing me that I'd been there a month. Maybe that was because they usually count things in weeks in bureaucracy and he thought I was asking him to translate the hieroglyphics he'd been trained to read in my passport. My passport said I was going to Nepal to find a healer. I don't remember saying that but that does sound like something I'd say, doesn't it? The thing about temporary loss of time is that in a pinch you can pretend to be yourself.

So when I learned I now had some time, in fact that I could go wherever I wanted to go, I returned to the city where you live. I didn't know if I lived there, and apparently I don't live there now, but I knew you lived there and that I would return to see you for some reason I don't really remember right now. Which I did in a way, if only to find out who would remember me and where I lived, so I could accept or refute someone's notion of who I was and have somewhere to start or start again.

It turns out that I had lived with you and that you now lived with someone else. You both were very urgent that I take my belongings from the house so you could "get on with [your] lives." That made a certain amount of sense to me on some level, but on my level, which is only occasionally in step with other people's at any given time, I found myself wondering exactly how long I'd been gone and whether I could really rely on what one Nepalese Customs Agent had chosen to tell me.

You took great pains to explain everything to me, and then it was time to answer because the silence became very loud and neither one of us was doing anything about it. You had the questioning look on your face so I remembered my clues and acted like I was about to say something, because, of course, it was my turn.

I didn't say anything—I was thinking. I was thinking about what to say, and whether to tell you that I'd been to Nepal, and whether to tell you that I had lost time, and most of all I wanted to let you know that you'd made a mistake, because I had never lived there. And while I was thinking, you were standing on one foot and then the other, very uncomfortable I think the stance is. Probably you were imagining a lot of things going on my head that weren't really, I was just thinking. You were wriggling the same way you did that day I was shot.

We had parted on the street a few minutes before, habitually affectionate. Your face had rearranged itself for a parting even though you were confused about why things felt funny between us. But we had agreed not to bring up heavy things at dinner, because we had only an hour and it wouldn't be fair to throw out something for discussion that had a time limit on it. So an hour had come and gone and we were parting on the street and then I was shot.

I fell for a few hours, and people came from all directions for a few hours more, and I clutched my stomach after a day and a night had passed and realized that I was bleeding. It took you another few days to get to me and for that I was glad. I held the image of you between my teeth—you striding in wet cement from the corner to where I was still falling, your feet tracking great clumps of concrete with every stride. I chewed distractedly on the sight of you as blood rolled lazily down my belly, to my crotch, my thighs. Or else it was different—it may have spurted, with people playing out their separate versions of chasing the gunman, calling the police or tending to my wounds. In any case I watched you, drinking in every detail; your clumsy lope back to me, your normal grace completely supplanted by uncharacteristic terror. You turned, your weight on the wrong foot, as you saw me fall and you heard the shot—two separate, unrelated facts.

The light hung in sticky cobwebs; it was a time usually reserved for dusk. That day there was a clash—the sun didn't want to leave yet, the night was dallying somewhere in Japan, and the result was an uneasy meld of waxy yellow and timid blue. Like the day after a wildfire, fast and hot. Like the moment before the bomb, like a Santa Ana day, angry and strutting the streets looking for something to set ablaze.

You were stupid in slowness. There were people around me, people who had moved much quicker than you because they didn't know who I was. They didn't know, as you did, how I smell after a shower or that I play with the rings on my fingers when I'm nervous or how long it takes me to come. They hadn't been thinking about all those things together as they parted from me on the street just before nightfall, and none of those things was swirling in a weird mash in their heads as they kissed me on the mouth and strode away from me.

So it was terrific when I fell. It took a few hours to notice the smell of exhaust right there on the corner, to see the theater posters in the store window, to watch an old man wait for his dog while he looked up at the sound, to hear the shot reverberate in my head and then take its place in memory so I could play it over and over again. And you were stumbling through the crowd, through them to me. You dipped your hand into my belly with all the familiarity due you, both our faces bursting with satisfaction as the hand came up bloody. Blood was everywhere, actually, and inside I enjoyed a good smirk at your discomfort. You never did like blood, mine especially, and you did very well, it should be said, you behaved as if you had no history of blood-hating at all; you neither noted nor ignored it. It turned out to be a good thing I was smirking, as we learned later; it was crucial that I stay conscious right at that point. I forget why. So the slow motion of your gait was an easy distraction, occupying me for the requisite hours I needed to fill while we all waited for the ambulance. I watched as your body caught up with your soul, right there on the sidewalk, as you became yourself again and finally pushed the people away with your customary surety.

And at the very same time as you were becoming yourself again and I was watching you do so I felt the hole in my belly, wide-ripping to my backbone, white hot and past any kind of normal into an orgy of pain. I was safe again, as I had been only a few minutes before when I could fall and watch you run to me. I was safe again because you were becoming you once more and I was becoming something else, too; it was out of my hands. I was shot in the belly, lying on a gritty sidewalk with thousands of witnesses whom I could call up later when you took it into your head to testify, raging on the stand, that I had made up the whole thing. I saw your hand wet and dripping with my blood, saw you shout for a doctor, I saw you stand up and crouch back down to me, I saw you moving, slowly and without reason, I saw you move quickly, I saw you hovering around me, I saw you at the scene of the shooting, I did; I saw you there.

contributors

DIANA ABU-JABER was born in New York and raised between Amman and America. She completed her Ph.D. at SUNY-Binghamton and has taught at the University of Michigan, University of Oregon, and UCLA. Her first novel *Arabian Jazz* won the 1994 Oregon Book Award and was a finalist for the PEN-Hemingway award. Her forthcoming novel *Memory of Birth* won an NEA, and is due out from Norton this year. She recently wrote and produced an hour-long docudrama for NPR called "The Language of Peace." Currently living in Portland, she writes book and film reviews for *The Oregonian* and other publications, and is the Writer-in-Residence at Portland State University.

An artist and writer, MEAGAN ATIYEH left New York to return to her native Portland. This is her first publication.

BRIAN CHRISTOPHER's most recent collections of poems are *The Detective Poems, Angels In Exile,* and *Skin,* and he recently completed work on a novel, *Hard Heaven.* His short fiction, poetry, and essays have appeared in numerous magazines around the country and abroad, including: *Quarterly West, Santa Barbara Review, The Chariton Review, Exquisite Corpse, Global City Review, two girls review, Still, First Intensity, Lilliput Review, Hardboiled, Anodyne, The Maverick Press, Texture, Portland Review,* and *Blue Satellite.* He is the editor and publisher for Quiet Lion Press and the national literary magazine *Rain City Review,* and has lived in Oregon since 1976.

PAULA COOMER was born in Louisville, Kentucky. She is a former public health nurse, having worked many years on Idaho Indian reservations before leaving to become a writer. She holds an MFA in Creative Writing from the University of Idaho. The mother of two teenaged sons, she teaches at Washington State University, and is currently working on a memoir about her years on the Nez Perce Indian Reservation. This is her first published story.

COLIN DICKEY, on leave from Portland, is currently pursuing his MFA in Writing at California Institute of the Arts. "Seeking Ursa Minor" is part of a novel-in-progress and his first published work of fiction.

TREVOR DODGE has published fiction, interviews, and reviews in such print and on-line magazines as *Alt-X, Rain Taxi, House Organ, Sugar Mule, Review of Contemporary Fiction, American Book Review, Puck,* and *Carbon 14*. Since 1995 he has curated *Oblivion* (http://acker.thehub.com.au), an electronic repository dedicated to the work of Kathy Acker. He lives and teaches in Boise.

LEON JOHNSON designs and produces media communications and events. Exhibitions have included "Transcending Limits: Beyond Mainstream and Margin," touring nationally through 2001, and recently he performed "Empire Postcards" in the U.K. at the University of Coventry. Awards have included a Pollock/Krasner Foundation Award for painting, a Yaddo Residency Award, the Iowa Arts Fellowship and The Ersted Award for Distinguished Teaching. Leon is a professor at the University of Oregon, in Fine and Applied Arts. CHRISTOPHER BIDDLE studied filmscoring at Berklee College of Music, filmaking at the School of the Museum of Fine Arts, Boston and writing at the University of Massachusetts. In 1998 Christopher and Leon conducted a psychogeographical journey through London culminating in St. Nicholas Churchyard, Deptford, the site of Christopher Marlowe's murder and burial. That journey laid the foundation for the *FAUST/FAUSTUS* performance. In the Spring and Summer of 2000 they will perform the piece in Portland and London.

RICHARD KRAFT is an installation artist whose work has exhibited regionally and nationally, with upcoming shows at the Greg Kucera Gallery in Seattle and the Bemis Foundation in Nebraska. He chairs the photography department at the Pacific Northwest College of Art in Portland. He is the recipient of awards from the Oregon Arts Commission, the Regional Arts & Culture Council, among others. L.N. PEARSON's fiction has appeared in several anthologies. She's received fellowships in literature from the Oregon Arts Commission, Literary Arts, Inc., and others.

MICHAEL KROETCH recently finished a novel, *Blood Engines,* and two new short story collections, *Waking the Dead,* and *The Cousin Stories.* Five of his videos and two of his plays have won national contests, and he's a recipient of an NEA fellowship. You've probably seen him on TV—he's the guy that entertains himself by walking through traffic wearing a blindfold.

STACEY LEVINE is the author of *My Horse and Other Stories* and *Dra—*, both published by Sun & Moon Press. Her story collection won the 1994 PEN/West Fiction Award. She was born in St. Louis, and lives in Seattle where she writes for *The Stranger* weekly, *nest—a journal of interiors* and other publications. She is at work on a 2nd novel.

BILLIE LIVINGSTON's first novel, *Going Down Swinging,* will be published by Random House Canada in January, 2000. Her poetry and fiction have appeared in *The Malahat Review* and *Prism International* in Canada, *Imago* in Australia, and *Poetry Ireland.* A recent winner of the "Other Voices" tenth anniversary fiction contest, she lives in Vancouver, BC.

THE LA PUSH, WA EXPERIMENTAL WRITING & TYPING CLUB writes stories collectively on typewriters. JOHN DOWNS is blah blah blah. He had blah blah blah. He has appeared in *Blah.* SARAH TAFT will be back in five minutes. KATIE HOFFER is the author of several unpublished cookbooks. JAN WALLACE is a Disaster Awareness Spokesperson and Metaphysician making blood money on the Selling Floor. MATTHEW STADLER writes novels.

JUDY MACINNES JR is the author of three chapbooks *Super Socco and Other Super Stories* (Ga), *Bearing Fur or Otherwise* (Ava) and *Black Footed Ferret is a Meat Eater* (Tiny Bat Books). Her writing has been anthologized in *Breathing Fire: Canada's New Poets* and *Eye Wuz Here: Women Writers Under Thirty* and has appeared in small Canadian magazines such as *Room of One's Own, CV2, Geist, Prism International, Blood & Aphorisms, The Capilano Review, Prairie Fire,* and *sub TERRAIN.*

DOUG NUFER became an editor of the *Washington Free Press* and *American Book Review* to do penance for all the grief he gave editors as a contributor to *The Stranger, S.F. Bay Guardian, Sports Illustrated* and *The Tentacle.* Formal constraints drive most of his fiction. An excerpt of his novel *Never Again,* in which no word appears more than once, was published in the *Oulipo Compendium* edited by Harry Mathews. He lives in Seattle.

LANCE OLSEN is the author of a dozen books of and about postmodern fiction, including the novel Tonguing the Zeitgeist and the first full-length study of William Gibson. His short story collection, Sewing Shut My Eyes, will be published by FC2 in 2000. He teaches in the MFA program at the University of Idaho. ANDI OLSEN's computer generated collages and assemblages have appeared in journals and shows around the country and abroad. Check out Café Zeitgeist at www.uidaho.edu/~lolsen.

ALLISON OWENS grew up in New Mexico and is now working at a bakery in Missoula, Montana, where she lives with her husband, Matthew. This is her first publication.

CHUCK PALAHNIUK's first novel *Fight Club,* winner of the Pacific Northwest Booksellers Association Award and the Oregon Book Award for best novel, was sold in seven foreign markets and is now a major motion picture.

His most recent novel is *Invisible Monsters*. Palahniuk is a graduate of the University of Oregon and he lives in Portland.

VIRGINIA PATERSON is a writer living in Portland. She is pursuing graduate work and web design while doing social work at a battered women's shelter. She is hungry, aching, open, tasty, angry and laughing.

DAVID PINSON is a Portland writer. His fiction has appeared in *The Quarterly*, *Rain City Review*, *ZYZZYVA*, and *Plazm*, among other literary publications. He works for a major industrial corporation and is a graduate student at the University of Portland.

SHAMINA SENARATNE writes and performs in British Columbia. Her fiction and poetry is published in Canadian literary journals and in the anthology *Seven Sisters: Writing from the Seven Sisters Writing Group*, launched at the 1998 Vancouver International Writer's Festival. "Crossing the Marimba" is inspired by her experience composing electroacoustic scores and her love of jazz. Shamina is currently collaborating with Coriograph Theatre in Vancouver, developing dramatic text and narrative for a new modern dance show to be staged in 2000.

STEVEN SHAVIRO teaches at the University of Washington and is the author of *Doom Patrols* (Serpent's Tail, 1997) and of *Stranded in the Jungle* (currently being published serially on the World Wide Web at http://www.dhalgren.com/Stranded/index.html.

ELIZABETH SHÉ is the author of *Shoulds are for Saints: the true life adventures of Suzy Le Speed*. She lives in Washington, where she's learning to fly jets. Shé is the former editor and publisher of *MEOW*, an arts journal. Mainie Jellett (1987-1944) was an almost mathematically precise Irish Cubist painter. "Listening to Mainie Jellett" was written in response to her painting "I Have Trodden the Wine Press Alone."

DAVID SHIELDS is author of the novels *Dead Languages* and *Heroes*; a collection of linked stories, *A Handbook for Drowning*; and two works of nonfiction, *Remote* and *Black Planet: Facing Race During the NBA Season*. His stories and essays have appeared in the *New York Times Magazine*, *Harper's*, *Vogue*, *Details* and the *Village Voice*. The recipient of fellowships from the National Endowment for the Arts fellowships, the PEN/Revson Foundation and the New York Foundation for the Arts, he lives with his wife and daughter in Seattle, where he is a professor of English at the University of Washington.

CAITLIN SULLIVAN writes for the artistic and transgendered communities, and co-wrote the novel *Nearly Roadkill: an Infobahn Erotic Adventure* with Kate Bornstein. She has written several plays, works free-lance as a journalist, and searches for patrons who will indulge her love of travel and slacking. While waiting, she lives in Seattle, where she alternates working for evil corporations and artistic projects. She is working on a second novel.

BRIGID YUKMAN, poet, lives in Seattle. She is working on two books of poetry, *Lives of the Puzzleworkers* and a new manuscript. Her hands are fiercely tender in their makings. She is a practicing psychodramatist.

LIDIA YUKNAVITCH is a writer.